Vicki's Vows
Book 6 in Clover Creek Community
Kirsten Osbourne

Copyright © 2023 by Kirsten Osbourne
Unlimited Dreams Publishing
All rights reserved.

Cover design by Erin Dameron Hill/ EDH Graphics

No part of this book may be reproduced in any form or by any electronic or mechanical means including information storage and retrieval systems, without permission in writing from the author. The only exception is by a reviewer, who may quote short excerpts in a review.

This book is a work of fiction. Names, characters, places, and incidents either are products of the author's imagination or are used fictitiously. Any resemblance to actual persons, living or dead, events, or locales is entirely coincidental.

Kirsten Osbourne
Visit my website at www.kirstenandmorganna.com

Chapter One

Spring, 1856

Vicki Abigail Williams looked up when the front door opened. She was cooking supper for her family, and her mother and sisters were out planting the kitchen garden. Spring had come early there in Clover Creek for the first time since they'd settled there.

To her surprise, it was Abigail Appleby. "Hi, Abby."

"Vicki, I wanted to let you know that the people who came back together, my best friend, Anna, and John among them, are finally here. I'm sure it'll be a few days before they're ready to talk to people, but they're here. Thought you might want to know."

Two marriages bound the Applebys and the Williams families, which made all of the Applebys feel like family to Vicki, though they really weren't. "That's nice," Vicki said, trying to sound casual as her heart jumped in her chest. She and John had talked for a long while when their company had been there in the fall. "I'm sure you're thrilled to have Anna back here."

Abigail nodded. "I've never gone a full six months without seeing her before. I'm so glad she's here." "I can't wait to share my life with her."

Vicki smiled. "I'm so happy for you." *And me. I'm happy for me. John is back!*

"It's Friday, so I think they'll be at church Sunday. It's going to be hard, but I'm not going to try and see Anna before then. If she comes to me, that's one thing, but I won't go to her."

Vicki nodded. "That makes sense. She'll be putting in a garden, I would think."

Abigail nodded. "We spent the morning planting a garden ourselves. I should get back to it with the others, but I wanted to let you know because you seemed to be sweet on John."

Vicki blushed. "I wouldn't say sweet on him." *I'd say I'm madly in love with him and want to have his babies.*

"I see," Abby said. And from the look on her face, Vicki knew she was completely aware of her feelings. "Okay, I'll get back to gardening then."

Vicki finished peeling the potatoes for the stew she was making and then dumped them into the pot with the carrots, onions, and beef. She'd already browned the beef, and she added water and seasoning and moved the pot to the center of the stove.

Then she went back outside to help with the garden. She'd go in every thirty minutes or so and make sure everything was cooking well, but she had to put in time working on the garden as well.

Vicki joined her mother and younger sister Barbara in the garden and took a bag of carrot seeds to plant. "The strawberries look good," Vicki said. They would be the first fruit to pick and put up that year. She preferred gardening to cooking and sewing, but thanks to her sister-in-law Henri, she was now adept at cooking, and with her mother, she'd always been adept at sewing. She just preferred outdoor work to indoor, so she was happiest in the garden.

"They do," Ma agreed. She wasn't one who enjoyed gardening, but she did it because her family liked to eat, and this was the only way to get fresh produce. Of course, they'd have to can a lot of it before long so they could make it through the winter.

Sometimes Vicki thought that all they did was prepare for winter, but if it made it so they could be comfortable, then it was worth it. She was happy growing carrots and everything else the garden would hold that summer. Then in the winter, she'd be making jerky and putting up the meats the men brought in. Henri, her brother Roy's wife, had taught her how to make meat last as long as possible, and she was thrilled to have the knowledge.

Her parents were the proud owners of a cattle ranch, along with her brother. They had claimed land beside one another so there would be more land for their venture. She liked to imagine what it would be like when she had her own homestead, and she shared a home with her husband, whomever he may be. Though she had to admit if only to herself that the future husband's face had become John's in the past few months.

He wanted to start a farm in the valley, which she didn't know a great deal about, but she was willing to learn. There was good land all over. Perhaps he would choose to be a bit closer to the lake than she was with her parents. She couldn't imagine not seeing her family on a daily basis, but perhaps it would be good for her to be more independent.

She had gotten used to cooking since they'd settled in Clover Creek because Henri had taught them all how to cook. Ma couldn't cook to save her life, but she made the best jerky around. Vicki had learned to make jerky from her mother, and she knew she did a good job of it. She would continue to follow her mother's receipt once she was married.

All she could think about was John being back in their community. Oh, how she wished she could hurry him into marriage, but she also wasn't sure that was wise. She would just make herself available for courting and see what happened from there.

John had promised to come back and settle in their valley so he could get to know her better. Surely that meant he was as interested in a marriage between them as she was. At least she hoped it did. Life got more confusing as you got older, it seemed.

After planting her row of carrots, she hurried back into the house to check her stew, and gave it a few good stirs. Their first year in Clover Creek had been spent in a small log cabin. Thankfully two of her siblings had moved out immediately, but that was still leaving four people in a small cabin. Two years before, her father had built them a real house, and for the first time in her life, she had her own bedroom.

She hurried back out and was given a bag of potato quarters, which she immediately began planting. Putting in a kitchen garden would take her, her mother, and Barbara at least a week. It was a lot of work, and Vicki was just glad she loved it so much.

She was bent over putting a potato quarter into the hole she'd just dug and covering it with dirt when a horse and rider stopped in front of the house. She was wearing her bonnet, but still needed to shade her eyes to see who was there. Once she realized who it was, her heart stopped for just a moment.

She set the bag of potatoes down and walked to John, who was dismounting from his horse. "John! You're back. Did you get land around here?" Vicki asked. She was thrilled to see him.

He nodded. "I did. It's out closer to the lake. Most of the land immediately surrounding the town is gone."

"I'm sure it is," she said. "We have at least thirty companies coming through every year, and they each have around thirty wagons. It makes sense to pick a spot near a growing town."

He nodded. "I wondered if we could go for a walk."

She bit her lip. "Let me ask my ma. We're supposed to be putting in our kitchen garden, and I'm cooking supper as well."

"Let me just help with the garden then. I know I shouldn't have come over quite so soon, but I was hoping to see you, and make sure the beauty I remember is just the same."

She smiled. "And?"

"You've exceeded all expectations."

"Come meet my ma." Vicki walked toward her mother, who had stopped planting to watch her with John. "Ma, this is John. I met him in the fall. He was part of Abby's wagon train."

Ma smiled. "It's nice to meet you. I hope you'll enjoy living in Clover Creek."

"He's going to be a farmer here."

Ma nodded. "And you want to court my daughter?" she asked, making Vicki blush. Her mother could be so blunt at times when a little finesse was called for.

John nodded. "Yes, ma'am, if that's all right with you."

"You'll have to ask my husband, but you can stay for supper tonight if you'd like. Abigail cooked, so I'm certain it will be good."

"That would be nice," he said with a smile.

"Are you going to come back in an hour or stay here?"

"If you don't mind, I'll help Vicki with the planting."

Ma nodded, and went back to work, but Vicki knew her ma was watching her.

As they walked back to her bag of potato quarters, he frowned. "Isn't your name Victoria?" he asked.

She nodded. "Most folks call me Vicki, but my family calls me Abigail, which is my middle name."

"Ahh...so would you rather I called you Abigail or Vicki?"

"I prefer Vicki." She picked up the bag of potatoes, realizing then her backside had been in the air when he'd rode up. Apparently, it hadn't bothered him enough to say anything.

As they worked, she asked him about his plans. "Are you going to be a crop farmer? Or a dairy farmer?"

"Dairy. I brought eight cows with me, and one bull. Should be enough to at least get started. All eight cows are expecting any day."

She smiled. "That's a lot of milk right there. You'll build up your dairy quickly, I'll bet."

"I hope so. You have a doc in town, right?"

She nodded. "We do. He's good too. I've had to see him for the flu."

"Glad to hear he's good. I want to be able to go for him if one of the cows gets in trouble nursing."

"Yeah, I've heard he's good with animals as well, but since I'm not an animal, I have no way to be sure."

He chuckled. "Glad to hear you're not an animal."

She grinned. "I'm glad you chose to settle here. It's a good community, with good people. It's not big yet, and I hope it never is, but it's big enough. We have a store, and a sawmill, and even a boarding house."

He nodded. "I'm staying in the boarding house until I have my house finished. I'm going to build a little one-room house over a cellar, and then when I want to expand, it'll be easy."

"You're not starting with a log cabin?" she asked, surprise coloring her voice.

"I don't want to put that kind of effort in twice. I started the cellar yesterday, as soon as I got here, and I ordered my lumber from the sawmill. The food at the boarding house is excellent, so I'm eating most of my meals there. Mrs. Prewitt even packs me a lunch when I say I'm working all day. She's a nice lady."

Vicki nodded, smiling. "I don't know her well, but my interactions with her have all been good."

"I'm not surprised. Her little girls are just delightful."

Vicki nodded. "I've spent more time with her girls than I have with her. We all walked the trail together, of course, and the girls would sometimes find us and walk with us. It was fun to see them. I was only fifteen then, and Barbara was only twelve."

"Barbara is your sister?" he asked. "Is she the one I met?"

Vicki shook her head. "Okay, here's where it gets a little confusing. My older brother married the only girl from the Appleby family. Then my older sister married the oldest boy from the family. They live right above us on the hill, so we've sort of become just one big family in some ways. The girl you met was Abby, who was part of your wagon train, and she married the youngest of the Appleby boys."

"Oh! So she's not related to you at all?"

"Not at all. But it feels like she is in some ways, if that makes sense at all. When we do a big family meal, both families and all offspring show up. Usually, Henri cooks though. She taught me to cook, but my ma's cooking is terrible."

"I heard that!" her ma yelled back at her.

"Am I lying?" Vicki called back.

"She's telling you the truth," Barbara called. "But Ma makes the best jerky in the whole area."

"Jerky?" he asked. "I had a lot of jerky on the trail, but it's always been one of my favorite things." He looked at Vicki with his head tilted to one side. "Does that mean you make good jerky?"

She nodded. "Almost as good as Ma's."

John smiled. "I'll have to sample it one day."

Vicki nodded. "I need to run in and make sure the stew isn't burning. Come with me, and I'll get you some."

He didn't have to be told twice. "I'm working hard to get my house ready. I hope I can marry once it's done. You know anyone in the area who wouldn't mind marrying a farmer?"

She grinned at him but shook her head. "Don't know anyone at all. I hope you can find someone."

"I hope I can too. Having a wife to cook and clean for me would be wonderful."

"And garden," Vicki said. "I do love to garden."

"Really?" he asked. "That could be helpful too. But can you sew?"

She nodded, holding her arms out to each side. "I made this!"

"That's beautiful. You really can sew!"

"My ma makes up for her lack of ability with cooking with her sewing. She's the best seamstress around."

"I can see that," he grinned.

She went to the large jar that held some jerky, which was always kept filled and put some in a small cloth sack. "There. Now you know how good I am at making jerky, and since you're staying for supper, you can try my cooking."

"That sounds good to me. If your pa agrees, I want to court you."

She smiled. "I'd like that a lot."

"Really?" he asked. "I won't have a lot of time as I build my house and barn, but I'd love to see you whenever I can."

"Of course," she said. "I've been hoping you'd make it back to Clover Creek and be able to settle here."

"I was too. I was a little dismayed when I saw that all the plots of land close to town were taken, but I liked my proximity to the lake. I'll have better access to water for my cattle."

"I can't wait to see your land."

"Perhaps your pa will let me drive you out there after church on Sunday. We could stop at the boarding house for lunch and then drive out to see what I've done so far on my property."

"I'm pretty sure he'll allow it. Once he's spent a little time with you, he'll know you're safe for me to be alone with."

John liked that idea. He couldn't wait to talk to her father.

Chapter Two

When Pa got back from his day on the ranch, he studied John for a moment. "You've settled here?" he asked.

John nodded. "Yes, sir. I met your daughter Vicki back in October, and I'm hoping you'll allow me to court her."

"I don't know you," Pa said. "Can't say yes or no, until I do."

"Your wife invited me to supper. Perhaps you can get to know me as we eat," John replied.

Vicki held her breath as she watched the exchange. Her pa came across as gruff, but inside, he was as soft as a dandelion.

When everyone sat down to supper, Vicki was glad she'd cooked. Any man who tried her ma's cooking would run as fast as he could away from her. She'd even baked bread that day, so he could try her fresh bread, which always turned out well.

Pa said the prayer, and then Ma served him, John, herself, and the two girls. Vicki quickly took her first bite of the stew, praying it had turned out well. When it was good, she sighed happily.

Ma buttered bread for everyone, asking how many pieces people wanted. Her pa always asked for four because he had gone years and years without bread thanks to Ma's inability to cook.

Once John, who sat beside her on the bench that had been made for her and her sisters, had his bread and stew, he dipped a small piece of the bread into the stew and took a bite. "This is delicious," he said.

Barbara nodded. "Only because Ma didn't cook. Abby always cooks now because she's the best cook in the house."

Ma frowned. "Everyone was happy with my cooking until Henri made a meal for us. Then they all wanted me to cook like her. I can cook a few more things than I could before, but the girls have really done well with their cooking."

Vicki didn't meet John's gaze, but she was inwardly delighted at the praise. "I made pie tonight too," she said softly.

Barbara grinned. "I love your pie."

"You just love pie," Vicki responded.

John smiled at Barbara. "I'm with you. I love pie."

"No one loves it as much as Bastian," Barbara said. "I'm surprised he hasn't turned into a giant pie. Ma always says you are what you eat. Though, we should have all been giant hunks of burnt, dried-out meat, if that was true."

Pa looked at Barbara. "That's enough. I'd rather not hear anyone make fun of my wife's cooking. She kept us all alive."

"That's true," Vicki said, ready to stick up for her mother.

"What are you planning on farming?" Pa asked John.

John nervously swallowed before answering. "Dairy cattle," he said quickly. "I have eight cows to start and one bull. I expect to have many calves in the next few weeks."

"Sounds good. And your plot is out near the lake?" Pa asked.

John nodded. "It's a thirty-minute drive, but I'll come into town often, especially for church."

Pa nodded. "Glad to hear you're a church-going man. Have you started your cabin yet?"

"I've started the cellar for the house I'll build, and I've ordered the lumber from the lumber mill. Until I get it built, I'm staying at the boarding house Margaret Prewitt runs. She's an excellent cook."

"And you came into town to visit a young lady before you had the cellar built?"

"I wanted to make sure Miss Vicki knew I was back here and she didn't agree to court anyone else. I'll spend the rest of the week finishing up the cellar and then start building. I need to build a house, barn, and fences."

"Many around here don't bother with fences. They just make sure they have their cattle branded so we know who it belongs to. You're in a community full of Godfearing men and women. There's no danger of cattle being rustled."

"Glad to hear it. I'll do that then. Maybe the fences can wait."

"I'd sure build the barn before fences," Pa said. "Your cattle will need a warm place this winter."

"Yes, sir. I'll make sure I do that."

"And you want to court my Vicki…"

John met Pa's eyes straight on. "I would very much like your permission to court her."

Pa thought about it for a moment. "I think that'll be fine. Don't keep her out late, and make sure you always tell me where you're going."

"I'd like to take her for a drive after church on Sunday. I want to show her my land, and take her to lunch at the boarding house."

Pa nodded. "That'll be fine. Eat most of your meals with us though. No use wasting money that you don't have to spend."

"Thank you, sir."

After supper, John took her for a walk. "I just wanted to spend a little bit of time alone today. Your sister does the dishes?" he asked.

"Since I cooked, Ma will wash while Barbara wipes. If Barbara had cooked, I'd be washing and Ma would be wiping. We try to keep the work fair to all of us."

As soon as they were out of view of the house, he took her hand. "Do you mind?" he asked.

She shook her head. "I don't mind at all." Her mother had always been very open with her and her sisters about the marriage bed and what to expect. It sounded like something wonderful to hear Ma tell about it, and she didn't feel shy about holding hands or even kissing. "Your family is back East?" she asked.

He nodded. "They are. In West Virginia. I finished school, and worked for the past six years as a coal miner. Because I lived at home, I was able to save up a good sum of money, and I used that to come West. Ma and Pa have eight other children, and they told me to live a good life. I'll be writing Ma this week to let them know I've made it to my destination and I'm starting to build."

"Just writing your ma?" she asked. That seemed weird. She knew she'd be writing a letter to the entire family.

"Pa doesn't read," he said softly. "So I'll write Ma, and she'll read it to all of them. It works that way."

"Sounds like it." She felt sad for his years in a coal mine. From what she understood, mining was difficult, dirty, and didn't pay well.

They reached a wooded area not far from the house, and she turned to him. "I know this will seem forward, but Ma has told me that touch is an important part of marriage. She said if you don't see fireworks in your mind when a man kisses you, he's not worth your time. So I wondered if you'd kiss me, so I could see if I see fireworks."

He chuckled. "I was walking along, holding your hand, wondering if you would be offended if I asked for a kiss. I guess not."

She grinned. "I don't believe I would be offended."

He leaned down and brushed his lips across hers, very gently. When he went to lift his head, she'd wrapped her arms around him and held him in place, and she deepened the kiss. Her tongue stroked against his lips and then just a bit inside.

He thought his body would explode at the touch of her tongue, and he opened his mouth to share a more passionate kiss. When he finally raised his head, he was out of breath, and more than a little aroused. This girl packed a punch.

She stood out of breath as well, just looking at him. "I think I saw so much more than fireworks."

He chuckled softly. "As did I. I don't think there's any worry about us being physically compatible."

"No, not at all," she said softly. "I wasn't expecting to feel quite so much." Her whole body felt differently as he'd touched it. Her nipples felt a bit sore and felt him all the way to her core. He was the right man. There was no doubt in her mind.

As they walked back, he still held her hand, and though it had felt exciting and new all the way to the wooded area, it now felt like it wasn't enough. He wanted more kisses, and he wanted a lot more than kisses. He didn't know if he'd be able to wait to make love with her until after their house was built.

"I'll spend all day tomorrow digging my cellar, and then I'll see you at church on Sunday, and we'll go for that drive after church."

"I'd like that a lot," she said, swaying toward him.

"If your pa sees me kissing you goodnight, will he come after me with a rifle?"

Vicki giggled. "No, he's very much like my mother about these things. He'd probably watch to see if he thought you were the right man for me."

"My parents were very different than yours," he said softly. "But if you don't mind…" He lowered his head to hers for another kiss, and Vicki wrapped her arms around him. When he raised his head, she looked as dazed as he felt. "I'll see you at church Sunday. Sleep sweet."

Vicki sighed happily. "You too."

"I'm off to milk the cows and then get to the boarding house. I'll be up extra early tomorrow so I can get that house built just as fast as I can."

"Sounds wonderful," she said softly. "Dream of me."

"I'm sure I will." But his dreams would likely not be the platonic dreams of a young girl like her. His dreams would be of their wedding night, and all he wanted to do to her body. It was hard to act like a gentleman when he wanted to do so much more with her than kiss.

She went inside and closed the door behind them, a smile on her face. She walked toward her bedroom, thinking of calling it a night, and she could dream of him. Oh, would she dream of him.

Her mother followed her into her bedroom. "That kiss looked like you are very happy with John."

Vicki turned her back to her mother to have her unbutton her dress. "It was wonderful. I want to marry him, Ma."

"And you met in the fall? Why haven't you mentioned him."

"I wasn't certain he'd really move here, even though he said he would. We talked for a few minutes one time. How was I to know he wanted to marry me?"

"He's mentioned marriage already?"

Vicki frowned for a moment thinking. "Yes, he has. For a minute I wasn't sure if he'd mentioned marriage, or if I'd just been thinking about it since he arrived."

Ma shook her head. "You are your mother's daughter. Will you see him tomorrow?"

Vicki shook her head. "No, not until Sunday at church. He's going to spend the whole day tomorrow digging his cellar. He said he wants the house done as soon as possible."

"You'll be able to marry faster," Ma agreed. "All right. Just making sure you have the feelings for him you think you have."

"Kissing him was like being in the middle of a war, with shots and cannons going off all around me," Vicki said.

"Then he's the right man for you. There's no question about it. I'll only have one baby left at home by fall, I guess."

"That baby is growing up fast," Vicki said. "She's only three years younger than me."

"Don't remind me. I can't believe how quickly you're all marrying and moving out."

"It's time," Vicki said. "John is the man I've been waiting for."

"Good. Then I won't have to worry about you going for that ride with him on Sunday. Just remember, keep your legs closed until you have made your vows in front of the preacher."

Vicki nodded. "I will. Though, I have a feeling, it won't be easy."

Vicki climbed into bed and though she'd always tried to be a good girl, her mind went to the man she'd spent her evening with. John. He was everything to her. Her present and her future.

She pulled out her journal that she denied keeping to her sister Barbara, who was always looking for it to read. She kept it under her mattress though. She carefully wrote the day's date.

April 20th, 1856

John has settled here in Clover Creek. Well, near Clover Creek. He came today, to tell me he was here, and to ask my pa to allow him to court me. Pa wasn't here, so he stayed for supper and Pa agreed after talking with him for a while.

And then John took me for the most heavenly walk. Or maybe it was a sinful walk? I suppose it depends on who you ask. He held my hand until we reached the woods, and there I asked him to kiss me. I know it was brazen, and forward, and all the other things girls aren't supposed to be, but I wanted to be sure we were physically compatible before we married.

His kiss made me see not only fireworks but an entire display of all of the most advanced weapons. He's the man for me. I just know it. Tomorrow, he'll spend the entire day digging the cellar for our house, and then Sunday, we'll see one another at church, and go for a drive after church.

I do hope he'll sit with my family. I know Ma won't let me just up and sit with only him, but sitting with our family would be fine in her eyes. He plans to take me to the boarding house for lunch, and I've never had a meal that was paid for and not cooked by family or a friend, so that is very exciting. And then we'll go and see his homestead, and I'll get to see where I'll live for the rest of my life.

I'm going to marry John Abbott. You just wait and see.

She hugged her journal to her chest before tucking it away between her mattress and the wall, where it had been kept since the last time Barbara found it. As she closed her eyes, she imagined what her day out with John would be like. A whole day with the man she loved. What could be better than that?

She found herself a bit too excited to sleep. John was back in Clover Creek, and he still had feelings for her, as she did for him. She only prayed he could work quickly to get the house done. Vicki was more than ready to move in.

Chapter Three

By Sunday, John had his cellar dug out, and he'd gotten his first delivery of wood from the sawmill. He would be able to start building his home on Monday morning, and he was thrilled. It shouldn't take him more than two or three weeks to get the house built, and then he could marry Vicki. If her father consented, of course, but it seemed as if he would.

As he drove into town on Sunday, in his nicest clothes, he hoped that Vicki would be allowed to sit with him. He wanted everyone to know that she would be his.

When he arrived at church, she was already there, sitting with her mother. She spotted him, and smiled, which was a good sign in his mind. He walked over and smiled. "Would it be all right if Vicki sat with me?" he asked.

Her mother shook her head immediately. "No, our unmarried daughters sit with us," Ma said.

"Would it be all right if he sat with us? I could sit on the other end of the pew with him on the aisle. Please, Ma?" Vicki knew it was the best they could hope for.

Ma nodded. "Yes, but if I hear the two of you whispering even once, you won't sit together before you marry."

"Yes, Ma," Vicki said, knowing her mother meant every word. She scooted to the far end of the pew and when he sat beside her, she explained. "I knew she wouldn't let me sit away from the family, but I hoped the two of us would be allowed to sit together if we sat with the family. I hope that's all right."

"Definitely. I didn't realize such a small difference would change her mind." He took her hand and squeezed it, but promptly let it go when he saw her father looking at them.

She giggled. "My parents are really strict when it comes to what we do in church."

"I see that," he said. "I'm just going to sit here and be as well-behaved as possible," John said.

"I'm excited to go to the boarding house for lunch. I've never eaten anywhere but with family and friends. It'll be a new experience."

He nodded. "I think you'll like it."

"No doubt in my mind," she said.

"I'm excited to show you my homestead. There's not much there yet, but I think you'll like its proximity to Bear Lake."

"I know I will," she said, smiling at him. "We're talking like us getting married is going to happen, and we haven't even courted yet."

"I'll court you today, and marry you tomorrow," he said, winking at her.

She laughed. "I'm not so sure about that. I think we may need to court just a little longer to satisfy my family, but Emma and Jared didn't court long."

"Emma is your sister?" he asked.

She nodded. "The only one older than me."

"How long do you think your pa will want us to court?" he asked. "I think I can have the house built in a couple of weeks. Will your father be all right with that?"

"I think so. For our family, that's a long courtship."

He laughed at that. "I'm not going to worry then. I'll make sure we spend every Sunday together, and maybe I can go to your house for supper on Wednesday nights? Then I can see you twice a week. I hate that I can't make it more, but building the house needs to be my first priority."

"I agree, and I know my father does. Marrying once the house is built sounds wonderful."

The pastor made announcements after church that morning, and he said the annual spring dance would be held the next Saturday evening. "That means all you ladies need to make your best meals, and we'll eat together, and we'll have music and dancing afterward."

Vicki was excited. It would be her first time to be able to attend the dance with a beau. At least she hoped John would be able to take her.

As soon as the closing prayer was over, John looked at her. "Will you go to the spring dance with me?"

"I thought you'd never ask," she said, grinning.

He stood and spent a minute talking to her pa to be certain it was all right if he took her to the dance.

Pa nodded. "That would be fine. I'd like you to have Abby home by suppertime, and you can stay for supper if you'd like."

"Who's cooking?" John asked, a twinkle in his eye.

"Barbara. We do our best to be sure my sweet wife doesn't have to sweat in front of a stove."

"I'll have her back by six. Does that work for you, sir?"

Pa nodded. "Absolutely. Be good."

John offered Vicki his arm and led her out to his wagon. "We'll go to lunch first." He helped her into the wagon before running around and climbing behind the horses.

As he drove over to the boarding house, he grinned at her. "I'm excited to have a day to spend with you."

"I've been hoping you'd come back and court me since we met in October."

He nodded. "I've felt the same. I'm glad I'm here."

At the boarding house, he helped her down. "Mrs. Prewitt said to go on in, but lunch would take at least thirty minutes after she got home from church."

"That's fine," Vicki said. "I'm excited to spend time with you without my family watching over me."

They went inside and he chose a table off in one corner of the room. "This looks good to me."

She nodded. To her surprise, Jamie Prewitt, Margaret's husband, walked around with a pot of coffee and a pitcher of water, filling drinks for anyone who wanted them. "We're having beef roast for lunch today," he told them when he got to their table. "Would you prefer it as a sandwich, or on its own with carrots and potatoes?"

Vicki nodded. "I think I'd like it as a sandwich."

Jamie nodded. "We serve it open face with mashed potatoes on the side and gravy over all of it."

"Sounds delicious," Vicki said.

"I'll have the same," John said.

After Jamie left, Vicki asked, "Are all the meals here so fine?"

He nodded. "I've always loved chicken and dumplings, and I think Mrs. Prewitt makes the best chicken and dumplings I've ever tasted."

"I'll get Henri to teach me to make them, so you can have them at home too."

He smiled. "I'd like that a lot. And Henri is married to your brother?"

She nodded. "She and Roy married when we first settled here, and they have three small children now. She's expecting again, so she's exempt from garden duties."

"She doesn't work while she's expecting?" he asked, surprised.

"There are four families who share a garden up on the hill, and they are able to work around whoever is pregnant. Even their father, Mr. Appleby recently remarried and his wife had a child, but they don't think they'll have more children. Melody is already in her forties."

He nodded. "I guess if it works for them, that's good."

"I sure think so," Vicki said. "They enjoy one another's company a great deal. I feel left out sometimes."

"Have you asked to be included?" he asked, frowning. He didn't like the idea of her not being able to do what she wanted with people she cared about.

She shook her head. "No, I haven't. Ma needs me to help with the chores, and I just don't feel that I should stick my nose in where it doesn't belong."

"Do you know Anna and her husband?" he asked. "They were part of our company, and I know they know Abigail."

"Oh, she's Abby's best friend!" Vicki said. "I remember meeting her."

"Her homestead is right next to mine. They're dairy farmers as well. I think the two of you could spend time together after we marry."

She smiled. "I'd like that a lot. If she's friends with Abigail, then I'm sure we'll have fun together."

The food was just as good as he'd said it was. "This is delicious," she told Margaret when she came by to make sure they were happy with their meals.

Margaret smiled. "Thank you, Vicki. I do love to cook."

"You kept all the single men in our company alive on the trek here," Vicki said. "Even after you married you were still cooking for many of the men."

Margaret nodded. "I got free meat in exchange, so it all worked out."

After they'd left the boarding house, he pointed the horse in the direction of the lake. "Are you on this side of the lake or the other side?" she asked.

"This side, but just barely. I have to go the long way around."

She nodded. "All right. Let's go see this amazing property of yours." She loved to swim, and she almost told him that, but she was afraid to. She usually swam in her drawers, and her mother wouldn't like her telling him that.

As they drove, he talked about his family back in West Virginia while she discussed her grandparents back home. "Are you glad your family brought you all this way?" he asked.

"I didn't enjoy the walking as much as I could have, but I'm glad we're here now. Pa is able to do what he's always wanted to do. Back East he worked in a factory, which he hated."

"I feel the same. I have been saving to come out here for a long time, and I made sure I had some pocket money as well. Oregon Territory must be the most beautiful place on Earth."

"It is," she said. "I wouldn't go back East if you paid me. And I certainly wouldn't walk back East."

He shook his head. "I drove, of course, so I didn't spend nearly as much time walking as you did, but that journey was hard. I had someone ask me if I'd go back and bring another group out here as their captain, and I said no. It was too much, and I want to get my dairy farm off the ground."

"I'm excited to have Anna as a neighbor," she said. "I know she and Abby were always really close, and that means she's a good person, because Abby would never be friends with anyone who wasn't."

"Her husband is very nice," he said. "We worked together keeping watch over the herd a few times on the way out here."

"Did you travel with them back here from Oregon City?"

He nodded. "I did. It was nice to not have to travel alone. There were a couple of other wagons coming this way as well, and the four wagons followed each other. It felt so much safer."

"Did you have trouble?" she asked.

He shook his head. "I was warned that the Indians were riled up, and they would attack small parties, but it never happened. I don't know why they were even saying that."

"I'm just glad you didn't run into trouble," she said. "I would have been very sad if you hadn't made it back."

"It's very strange, this connection I feel to you," he said. "We spent twenty minutes talking to each other six months ago, and it's like we made a commitment to each other."

She nodded emphatically. "I feel the same way!"

"I guess we're just meant to be together," he said.

"We are," she told him. "I can feel it deep inside me."

He stopped in front of a huge hole in the ground not one hundred yards away from the lake. "This is my land," he said. "I'm building beside the lake because it will be easier to tote water, but my land stretches way out that way." He pointed south toward Clover Creek.

"I think you picked a very good spot," she said. "Anna and her husband?"

He pointed toward the east. "It won't even be a five-minute walk between our homes," he said, smiling at her.

"I'm so excited," she said. "I can't wait to get to know Anna, and I love your homestead. We'll have beautiful views of the lake every single day."

He nodded. "I think I picked a good spot. I'm really surprised no one took it."

"We all liked the Clover Creek area so much that we couldn't stray this far," she said with a smile. "I only wish I'd been old enough to get my own land. Then we'd have double."

"This land is plenty for my purposes. We don't need more. Maybe in fifty years we will, but I'd rather not even think about that now."

She took a step closer to him. "I think you should kiss me on the land we'll work together as husband and wife," she said softly.

"I'll kiss you anywhere and anytime you want," he said, lowering his head toward hers.

His kiss made her forget where they were, and why they were there. It truly made her feel like she was the most desirable woman in all of Oregon Territory.

When he lifted his head, she sighed happily. "Soon we won't have to stop, and we can really make love," she said.

He blinked a couple of times. "We shouldn't be talking about that," he said.

"Probably not, but only the two of us know. What difference does it make?"

"I suppose the world won't end." He walked her toward the bench he'd made. "This is going in front of the house," he said, sitting down, and patting the seat beside him. "You're not afraid of lovemaking?"

She shook her head adamantly. "My mother has always been very open about it," she said. "She's explained everything, and she calls it one of God's greatest blessings."

He shook his head. "My ma sure doesn't talk to my younger sisters about it that way," he said. "I think I like the way your ma does things better than mine."

She smiled, resting her head on his shoulder. "Me too. There's no reason for a young lady to be afraid of her wedding night. I'm thinking very positively about mine and wishing it could happen sooner."

"I'll build as quickly as I can. I'm sure looking forward to our wedding night as well."

She picked up her head and looked at John. "Are we engaged?"

"I would say we are," he said. "I'll talk to your pa and see if he'll give me permission to ask you."

"I think he will," she said. "He's ready to have one less mouth to feed."

"Has he said that?" John asked, surprised.

Vicki shook her head. "No, he hasn't said it, but each time one of my siblings marries, I can feel the difference in our family income. I think he'll be happy."

Chapter Four

On the way back to Clover Creek, they talked about their future and what each of them wanted. "I want at least a dozen children," Vicki said with a smile, looking off into the distance.

"I think five is enough for me," John said.

"Really? Don't farmers all want big families to help on the farm?"

He shrugged. "There were too many kids to feed in my family growing up. We did good to have meat on our table once a month, and the rest of the time, we ate beans."

"But it won't be like that for us," she said. "I'll always plant a good kitchen garden, and we'll always have milk. My family will share the meat they hunt, and I expect we will too. I've learned to feed a family on little because of the trail, and I'm sure I'll be able to do better than your ma did."

He nodded. "My ma never had a kitchen garden. We didn't live in a place with enough land for a garden. I think it was one of the ways the mine kept their people close. They didn't ever let people leave."

"That's sad. Did you feel like you were owned by the mine?"

"My pa did. All of the money he earned went right back to the company store for more money than we'd have paid anywhere else. But it was hard to get anywhere else because we weren't wealthy enough to have animals. When I started working the mine, I'd pay my ma ten percent of my salary, and the rest went to my savings. But I figured I owed money to the family for my keep. Even though I did share a room with my five brothers."

"That's a big family. Three sisters then?"

He nodded. "Ma always regretted when she was expecting. I was the oldest, and she cried on my shoulder more times than I could count." He shook his head. "I don't ever want you to be in a position where you start crying at the idea of having another baby."

"I don't see that happening, but once we have a few, we can make that decision," she said. She hadn't come from the kind of extreme poverty he was talking about, and she may feel more like he did later on. "What about the house? Do you want a big house or a small house?"

He shrugged. "I'll add on as we need to," he said. "Right now, I'm planning a house with one room, so the bedroom, kitchen, and dining room will all be one big room. Then as babies start to come, I can add on one room at a time."

"That sounds perfect. We spent our first winter here in a cabin, and it was four of us just like now. I do love having my own room now, though."

He smiled. "I'm sure you do. I love having my own room in the boarding house. I stayed in one in Oregon City as well, but it was the first time I'd ever had a room of my own. Very strange feeling."

"Maybe marrying isn't a good idea then..."

John's head whipped around as he looked at her. "Why would you say that?"

"Because then we wouldn't have our own rooms."

"Trust me, I'd rather share a room with you where we can make love as often as we want than have my own. Any day."

She smiled. "I like the sound of that."

"Good. Don't scare me like that."

Vicki laughed. "Sorry, but it was fun."

"So you like to tease, don't you?" he asked.

She nodded emphatically. "I love to tease. My family always teases each other. It makes me feel loved."

"I'll have to remember that."

When they reached her house, he quickly helped her down from the wagon and offered her his arm as they walked into the house. "Did you have a good time?" Ma called.

Vicki smiled and nodded emphatically. "Lunch was wonderful. I've always heard Margaret Prewitt was a good cook, and she definitely lives up to her reputation. I love his little homestead, which is right there on the banks of Bear Lake."

"That sounds lovely," Ma said. "I'm glad you had such a good time."

"Well, the company was wonderful, and that helped," Vicki said, smiling at John.

"It sounds like it," Ma said. "See if your sister needs help with supper."

Vicki nodded, hurrying into the kitchen. "Need any help?" she asked.

Barbara nodded. "I'm not as good about getting everything ready at the same time as you are," she said. "I have the chicken done, but the potatoes still need to be mashed, and I need to make gravy. Do you want to mash, or make the gravy?"

"I'll make the gravy," Vicki said, remembering how bad her sister's last attempt at gravy had turned out.

"Good. I hate making gravy."

"I kind of enjoy it," Vicki said honestly. "Not that I enjoy cooking a great deal, but you know what I mean."

Five minutes later, the gravy was made, and the potatoes had been mashed. Vicki carried a bowl of gravy to the table, noticing John was talking to her pa, which made her a little nervous. Barbara carried the potatoes to the table, and Vicki went back for the bread. Since Henri had taught Vicki and Barbara to make bread, they hadn't gone a night without it on their supper table.

When everything was ready, Barbara called the family to supper, and John came inside with a smile on his face. Vicki said a silent prayer that it meant that Pa had given permission for them to marry as soon as the house was built. Oh, how she hoped that was the case.

After the prayer, they passed the chicken around, and everyone filled their plates. "This looks really good, Barbara," Vicki said. "Almost good enough to eat."

Barbara stuck her tongue out at Vicki, and John laughed. "It's like being at home with my family," he said.

"How many siblings do you have?" Ma asked him.

"I'm the oldest of nine," he said. "My father is a coal miner in West Virginia."

"Coal mines are some of the hardest work there is," Pa said.

John nodded. "I mined for several years before I came West."

"I'm surprised you've been able to scrub off the coal," Pa said with a smile. "You must have left at least a year ago."

John smiled, nodding. "It took a good long while, that's for sure. For a while, I looked like a raccoon from the eye covering I wore down there."

Pa laughed. "I've heard of that. Glad I never had to do that job. I was a factory worker back East, and all I could think of was being a rancher. Thankfully my son Roy wanted the same thing, and we are working together to make it happen."

"Ranching is hard work too," John said. "I'm not sure I could do it. I'm very happy to have my small herd of cattle though. And one more heifer was born last night, so I have nine now."

Pa nodded. "Which is great. Every extra heifer you get will help. What are you going to do with the young males?"

"Castrate them and use them for food in the fall," John said. "From what I understand, my future wife has a good understanding of how to preserve meat."

Ma looked at Vicki and smiled, nodding. "She can do just about anything in the kitchen," she said proudly.

Vicki sighed. "Did I miss out on a marriage proposal just because my pa said yes?" she asked. "I think I deserve a proposal."

Barbara grinned, and clapped her hands. "Me too! I want to see it!"

Ma shook her head. "A proposal is a private matter, and Abby doesn't need her little sister watching."

"I always get confused when you call her Abby," John said. "To me she's always been Vicki."

"I don't remember why we started calling her Abigail, but it suits her. Victoria was my ma's name, and she died when I was little, so I wanted to have one girl named after her."

"I like to pretend that I was named after Queen Victoria," Vicki said. "Makes me feel like I'm more important than I am."

"You're a great deal more important to me than the queen," John said. "I wouldn't know her if I saw her."

Vicki smiled and squeezed John's hand under the table. "You're so sweet to me."

"I try," he said, grinning. "I'm building the house as close to the lake as I can without being in the flood zone. I don't want Vicki to have to walk very far as she fetches water for her chores."

Ma smiled at that. "I like that you're thinking of her, even before you marry."

"Oh, trust me. I am."

As soon as supper was over, John caught her hand. "We're going for a very quick minute, but then I'll bring her back so she can help with the dishes."

Ma nodded. "That would be appreciated. Barbara doesn't like to pull cooking and dish duty."

"No one does," Vicki said as she followed John outside.

"Thank you for a lovely day," John said, leaning down and kissing her softly. Then he asked in a low voice. "Will you marry me?"

"I would be delighted!" she said. "It's just nice to be asked."

He kissed her once more. "I'll be here for supper on Wednesday."

She nodded. "We usually eat at six."

"Sounds good. I'll see you then." With one more quick kiss, he climbed onto his wagon and drove away. She was glad he'd seen to the milking for the evening before they headed back to town. Now she knew he would only need to drive down to the boarding house that night.

She walked back into the house and immediately went to the kitchen. Barbara followed her in. "Well?" she asked.

"He asked me to marry him, and I said yes," she said. "He's hoping to have his house done in the next couple of weeks, and as soon as it's done, we'll speak our vows at the church."

"We need to make you a wedding dress," Ma said. She'd already boiled the water, so Vicki poured it into the sink and started washing the dishes. "I would like you to wear a white dress, just like Queen Victoria, but it's just not practical for a farmer's wife to have a white dress."

"I agree," Vicki said softly. "Maybe a dark blue? Or even a pink?"

"Pink would show more stains, but it would be a church dress for a few years before you'd wear it doing chores. I think pink would be fine, if that's the color you want."

"It is!" Vicki said. Pink had always been her favorite color.

Barbara stayed in the kitchen so she could discuss the wedding with her mother and sister. "Am I your bridesmaid? Please say yes!"

"I hadn't even thought about a bridesmaid," Vicki said. "Do you have time to make two new dresses, Ma?"

Ma nodded. "If you and your sister see to the garden, and all the cooking, I'll make sure that both dresses are made."

Vicki smiled. "Sounds like a good arrangement to me. And after I marry, I can put in a kitchen garden on John's homestead."

"I have extra seeds that we'll put in your hope chest."

Vicki had a real hope chest before they came West, but her father wouldn't agree to taking a chest for each of them, so they now had bags full of their hope chest belongings. "That would be wonderful, Ma. Thank you."

Ma nodded. "We didn't have time to do anything when we were planning Emma's wedding. It's going to be better this time. Two weeks is enough time for me to even plan a nice meal for anyone who comes to the wedding."

"Are you going to cook?" Vicki asked.

"Of course not. We'll call on the Appleby women to help us. You know they'll do it with smiles on their faces."

"Yes, they will," Vicki said, getting excited about having a wedding supper. "I want to serve chicken and dumplings."

Ma frowned. "Have you ever had chicken and dumplings?"

Vicki shook her head. "No, I haven't, but I know that they're John's favorite meal, and I want him to have it for our wedding supper."

Ma nodded. "That works. We'll get the receipt from Henri, and it will be fine. Now, do we want a wedding cake?"

Vicki thought about it for a moment. "I don't think so. It's a lot of work for whoever is making it, and I know it would be costly. Having the chicken and dumplings will be enough."

"We can ask some of our friends to bring bread as well, and then we can have bread with our chicken and dumplings."

Vicki nodded. "I think that's a great idea. I hate asking for favors, but that makes a lot of sense."

"Sounds good," Ma said. "And I'll make your wedding night nightgown like I did for your sister."

"I would love that, Ma." Vicki could remember the beautiful laced bodice nightgown her mother had made for Emma. She knew it would make John very happy to see her in it.

"Is there anything else you need?" Ma asked.

"Curtains and a tablecloth. I'm sure I can make them, but you asked, so I'm answering."

"That'll be easy. We'll wait until John finishes the house and builds your table. Then you can make sure to make them the right size. What are we missing?"

Vicki shrugged. "I'd like to spend a day with Henri and get her to give me receipts I can write down," she said. "That's the only other thing I feel like I'll need right away."

"That's easy enough. You know Henri will be excited to help. I'll make sure you take home some jerky, and some of the canned goods we put up from the garden last year."

"Oh, good," Vicki said. "I'll start a kitchen garden right away, but I won't be able to get any of the berries this year. Perhaps you'll share?"

"You know we will. I'm very happy for you, Abby. It seems to me like John is the young man you've been waiting for."

"I know he is," Vicki said with a smile. "I hate that we'll spend so much time apart for the next couple of weeks, but it makes sense that he has to focus on the house and not on me."

"The time will fly by because you'll be double busy at home," Ma said. "I'll make certain of it."

Vicki laughed. "That would be good. I know I need to stay busy so I don't think about him every minute of every day."

"Oh, you'll still think about him," Ma said.

Chapter Five

Vicki found herself living for the days she would see John. When he came to supper that Wednesday evening, he told her of the progress he'd made on the house. "The walls are up and the roof is on. I need to get a cookstove in there and make you a work table for the kitchen. And I need to make a table for us to eat at. I can make benches easily, but not chairs. Do you know of anyone who could make chairs for us?"

"Elmer King," she said automatically. "He's a furniture maker, and he's very good at what he does. I sleep in a bed he made."

"Wonderful! I didn't expect a furniture maker in a town this small."

"He's always busy," Vicki told him. "But he's really good. Our kitchen chairs were made by him. And he made Ma's kitchen cabinets."

"I wonder if he'd have any free time where he could come and work on cabinets with me," he said. "I'll find him and talk to him."

"I know he and his family live south of town, but that's all I know."

"I can figure it out from there," he said. "Thank you." He leaned down and kissed her since they were alone in the house. "Have you been busy this week?"

She nodded. "I've been doing Ma's portion of the chores as well as my own. Well, Barbara and I have split Ma's portion, but my sister does not move as fast as I'd like."

"Is your ma sick?" he asked, frowning.

She shook her head. "No, she's in the parlor making a dress for me for our wedding, and one for Barbara as well." She didn't mention there would also be a nightgown she was sure he would love because that was her surprise to him.

"Are you making chicken and dumplings for supper?" he asked, his face lighting up. "I can't believe I didn't notice as soon as I walked in the house!"

"I am. I've never had them, but Henri gave me her receipt, and I'm making the effort. Hopefully, by the time we marry, I'll be able to make your favorite meal."

He grinned. "Sounds delicious."

Her ma walked out of the parlor then, rubbing her eyes. "Dress is done," she said. "You should try it on later tonight." She smiled at John. "Good to see you."

He nodded. "I can't go for a full week without seeing my girl, so I'll be here on Wednesday nights for supper. I hope that's all right."

"It's very all right," Ma said with a smile. "We're happy to feed you whenever you want to come."

"Oh, I love your jerky!" John said. "Vicki gave me a bag of it, and it's wonderful. I've just about finished it off. It's perfect when I need a bite of food while I'm working on the house."

"I'm glad to hear it. Abby's jerky is every bit as good as mine," she said with a smile. "But she's a wonder in the kitchen compared to me. I'm proud of her for listening to Henri and applying everything she said."

Vicki smiled and kissed her mother's cheek. "Thanks, Ma. Cooking is a lot easier after all those lessons from Henri."

"You went for more than the rest of us if I remember correctly. You kept going when the rest of us stopped because you wanted to be able to cook for the man who would someday be in your life."

"And I'm cooking for him today," Vicki said, looking at John and smiling.

"And I sure appreciate all the effort you went to so you can cook for me. I'm really excited to try supper tonight. We'll see how it compares to my ma's."

Barbara hurried in from the garden, slamming the front door, and immediately calling out, "Sorry, Ma! The wind caught it!"

Vicki shook her head. "She says that every time she comes in because she always slams the door."

John chuckled.

Ma called to Barbara, "Come wash your hands. You can help your sister serve supper."

"Yes, Ma!" Barbara called back, just a bit too loud. Vicki loved her sister, but she needed to learn to be a bit less exuberant at times.

Vicki filled a bowl with the chicken and dumplings. She would have tried them, but she didn't really know how they were supposed to taste. Barbara washed her hands and carried in the stack of plates Vicki had set on the counter.

"Pa's not here yet," Vicki said, frowning.

"He's milking and then he'll be right in," Barbara told her. "I saw him as I was finishing planting the watermelon."

"Is that the last of the garden?" Ma asked.

Barbara nodded. "Finally. But it's been dry, so I think we'll need to start watering tomorrow." She looked exhausted at the very idea.

Vicki smiled. "You make supper tomorrow, and I'll do extra time in the garden."

"Perfect!" Barbara said. "I hate gardening."

"I love it. We'll get through this."

John liked how Vicki had just jumped in and offered to take on the burden her sister hated. He carried the bread into the dining room and set it on the table.

Barbara looked at him for a moment. "Why are you doing women's work?"

He shrugged. "It's how I grew up. All of us kids had the same chores to do, and we did them without complaining they were for the other gender. I can even cook some simple meals."

"That's different," Barbara said.

"I guess it is."

With the chicken and dumplings, Vicki had heated up some canned green beans and made several loaves of bread. "We're almost out of butter," Vicki told her ma.

"I guess that'll be one of your chores tomorrow, won't it?" Ma asked.

Vicki nodded. "Sure will." She didn't mind churning butter when she could do it on the porch. Then she was outside but doing work anyway. She hated to feel lazy, but always wanted to be outdoors. Something about the trail had changed her, making her want to spend more and more time in nature.

Ma looked at Vicki for a moment. "Would you like to take a rooster and five of my chickens?" she asked.

Vicki nodded. "I would love that! Ma is amazing with chickens," she told John. "You've never seen anyone who can do what she does. Every egg is double yolks. We'll be truly blessed to have some of her flock."

"Well, then I looked forward to taking some of your chickens."

"And I look forward to being able to take care of them. Another excuse to be outside."

John laughed. "You can always help me build the barn and the fences."

"I would," Vicki said, nodding.

He shook his head. "I don't think that would be wise. You're going to have enough to do to stay busy between tending the chickens and the garden, keeping the house up, and feeding me. Truthfully, feeding me might just be a full-time job."

Vicki smiled. "It's one I'm sure I'll enjoy." But she thought she might make a firepit to cook on. She wouldn't cook everything on it of course, but there were several things she knew would be fine over a fire.

"I plan to get a few hogs too, but I haven't had the chance yet."

"Talk to the Applebys," Ma and Vicki said at the same time.

"I will talk to the Applebys. Do they have more than they can use?"

"So many more," Vicki said. "The youngest son, Bastian, isn't great with people, but he is truly wonderful with animals. They've got quite a lot of hogs, and more every day. Maybe we can take a couple after they're weaned. I know Emma said their sow had ten pigs last week."

"Wow," John said. "I'd take two or three of them and we can have pork as well as the beef from the steers we butcher."

Pa walked into the house then, and they all sat around the table. After the prayer, John asked Pa about the hogs. "Do you think the Applebys would sell me a few hogs so I can start my own sounder of pigs?"

"I think they would. Jacob is always saying there are too many, and he doesn't want to build a larger pen. They use the hogs for food, but I don't think they usually sell them for the meat, so there's no reason to have so many."

"Would I talk to Jacob or Bastian?" John asked.

"I'd talk to Jacob. Bastian isn't the world's best conversationalist."

"Sounds good."

He noticed then that Vicki was watching him. "What?" he asked.

"I learned to make a new dish just for you, and I want to know if you like it!" she said.

"Oops. Sorry. Was excited about the prospect of hogs."

He stuck a fork into his chicken and dumplings and took his first bite. He closed his eyes and relished the taste. "Much better than my ma's. Maybe even better than Mrs. Prewitt's, but she could give you a run for your money."

Vicki smiled. "I'm so glad!" It would be a while before they had a chicken, she could butcher to make a dish like that, but she could always buy one from a neighbor.

"Very good job."

Ma smiled at Vicki. "My Abby sure can cook, can't she?"

Vicki wasn't so sure why her ma looked so proud that she could cook when she'd had nothing to do with it, other than teaching her the wrong way to do everything.

After supper, John looked at Vicki. "Since you cooked, you can walk with me, right?"

Vicki looked at her ma, who nodded. "Yes, I can."

As they left the house, John asked, "You seemed hesitant about whether you could walk with me or not."

"Ma is doing all the sewing, so she's been skipping household chores, but she said it was all right."

"Oh, I didn't think of that. Am I causing her too much work?"

Vicki shook her head. "She's the one who insisted on making me a new dress when I have a perfectly good Sunday dress I could marry in. I'm not worried. Ma would rather sew than do anything, but I could tell her eyes were bothering her earlier. It's probably good that she's taking a sewing break and doing something else."

"Sewing bothers her eyes?"

Vicki laughed. "If you do anything for a long period of time, something in your body is going to be bothered. As much as I love gardening, when I weed for hours, I get blisters on my fingers."

"I guess that's true." They'd reached the wooded area, which he was starting to think of as the kissing place. He pulled her into his arms and leaned down to kiss her, not asking permission this time because he knew her well enough to know she would always welcome a kiss.

When they parted, he sighed. "I want to kiss you when I wake up every day and before I sleep at night. I have to get that house finished enough that you can move in."

"I'd sleep under the stars with you," she said softly, moving in for another kiss. His touch ignited a fire inside her that she never wanted to go out. His hands roamed over her back and cupped her bottom, pulling her into him.

Finally, he groaned. "You're killing me, Vicki."

She sighed. "I just like it so much when you touch me and kiss me. Please get help and finish that house!"

"I'm glad I'm not alone in wanting to make love with you so much it hurts."

She nodded. "It's uncomfortable. I wish we were already married."

"I do too. But we're not." He sighed. "Let's walk back to the house and I'll say goodnight. Then I can be up before the sun tomorrow. I'll have breakfast and be at work by six-thirty or so. Now that everything is walled in, I don't have to wait for sun up, but I do need to wait for breakfast."

"I'll get you some more jerky," she said.

"I wasn't trying to get more jerky from you, but it would be appreciated. I want to get as much done as I can as quickly as possible. I wonder if your father would agree to let you marry me with no stove or really anything to cook on."

She giggled. "I know he wouldn't, but I like that idea."

He put his arm around her as they walked back up to the house. "I'll be here at five-thirty on Saturday night for the dance. I'm not a great dancer, but I'll do anything to spend more time with you."

"You are a good man, John. You make me feel like I'm something special."

He stopped walking. "Of course, you're special! Do not ever think you're not."

She shrugged. "I'm the middle daughter. Who cares about the middle daughter?" she asked.

"I do," he said. "I think you're very special. I saw you across the church, and I knew I needed to meet you. I thought of nothing but you after I left Clover Creek and came back here, so I could settle and have you for my wife. How could you possibly think you're not special?"

"I'm just not the best at anything. I'm a good cook, but not the best cook. I'm a good friend, but not the best friend. I'm a good gardener, but not the best gardener. I never seem to measure up to those around me."

"What if you're second best at everything?" he asked. "Would that work?"

She nodded. "I think so. I'm being silly. Don't mind me."

He hugged her to him and kissed the top of her head. "You'll be the best wife I could ever ask for. You'll be the best mother to our children. And you're going to be the best lover any man could ask for," he whispered.

She smiled up at him. "You might be right about all that."

At the house, he kissed her once more. "Five-thirty on Saturday night. Wear your dancing shoes."

"I have two pair, and they're both for dancing," she said.

He laughed and waved a hand in farewell. Vicki watched him drive away before going back into the house. "Can I help with the dishes?" Vicki called.

"They're finished," Ma said. "But go in your room and try on that new dress."

Vicki nodded, walking into her room. Instead of pink, her mother had made her a red and white gingham dress. It was absolutely beautiful, and she knew it would look perfect with her dark hair.

She quickly stripped down to her underwear and pulled the dress on over her head. It fit perfectly as all of the dresses Ma made did. She stepped out of her room and twirled so Ma could see it all.

"That looks very good." Ma stood up and walked toward her. "Not too snug, but not too loose either. I did make it so it could be let out for when you're expecting."

Vicki hugged her mother. "I love it, Ma."

Chapter Six

Vicki spent all day Saturday watching out the window and looking up every time she heard a sound. Barbara laughed at her as she finished watering the garden. "He said five-thirty. It's only two-thirty."

"I know! I know! But I want to see him. Yesterday would be good."

Barbara shook her head. "I never thought you would be so in love that you couldn't do your chores."

Vicki made a face at her sister, but her words made her think. Was she in love with John? She was definitely in lust with him, and she couldn't wait to be married, but was that just the lust, or was it because she was in love with him? She shook her head, refusing to dwell on it. John made her smile, and that was the most important thing in her eyes.

After the garden, she went inside to make supper. The dance was a potluck, as were all the meals in the community. It was her job to take enough to feed her family, and everyone would get whatever they wanted.

She decided to make a pot pie. If no one else would eat it, then Bastian Appleby would surely eat the whole thing. The man couldn't seem to live unless he had pie every day of his life, which amused Vicki a great deal.

She decided to make two pies. One would be a pot pie with chicken, and the other apple. Abby Appleby had been on a quest to can all the apples in the world last fall, and thankfully, she'd shared several jars of pie filling with her. Vicki was certain Bastian was still upset that he had to make do with fewer pies that year.

Vicki made both pies and put them both in the oven, sitting down at the table for a moment. It had been her first time sitting in hours.

Her wedding plans were coming together, though she hadn't confirmed a date yet. In a way, she wished it could just be her and John with the pastor, speaking their vows, but she knew her mother wanted to be there this time. When Roy and Emma had each had their weddings, they'd been brief with no family there. That seemed the best way to Vicki, but she knew her ma regretted the busy time they'd both married in. She'd wanted to be there to see her children marry.

She'd do as her ma wanted, as much as she wished things could be different. It would all be fine.

Vicki went into the parlor to check on her Ma, who had been sewing nonstop for a full week. "Anything I can do to help?" Vicki asked. "I watered the garden, and supper and dessert are both in the oven."

"You've been busy. Did your sister help with the garden?"

Vicki shrugged. "The same way she always helps."

"She's young," Ma told her. "She'll get better about doing her share of the work as she gets older."

Ma had been saying the same thing about Barbara for years. Vicki didn't agree with her, but she nodded anyway. "I hope so."

"Trust me. Without you here to bear the heaviest load, she'll realize how much you've done, and she'll have to step up and do more. It's that simple. You did the same when Emma moved out."

Vicki frowned. "I was never lazy like Barbara!"

"You were very similar to your younger sister until Emma married. Then you quickly took on more chores and more nights to cook. You're ready to be a wife now. Give your sister a few years to get to where you are."

"Yes, Ma."

Ma held up Barbara's dress. "What do you think?"

Her sister's dress was red, and it was a real lady's dress. Vicki realized it would be her sister's first dress to actually be fitted to her. "She's going to love it!" Vicki said, smiling.

Ma smiled. "I sure hope you're right!"

"Anything I can do to help you?" she asked. "With supper in the oven, I have to be indoors, but I've completed all my chores."

"That's good!" Ma said. "I don't guess there's a lot for you to do. Maybe you should take a little time to write in your journal."

"You know I still keep it?" Vicki asked, surprised.

"Your sister has told me often enough. Don't worry though. She can't find wherever you're hiding it now, and she's sure trying."

Vicki smiled. "I'll be happy when I don't have to hide it in this house anymore," she said. "I'll either keep writing in it after I'm married, or I won't. But either way, I won't have a sister trying to find it."

Ma laughed. "Barbara looks up to you. She wants to know all the little details about your life that you don't tell her. She's very curious about your relationship with John. We all are really. He seems to have come out of nowhere and appeared knowing he wanted to marry you."

"We really did meet in the fall. That last wagon train that came through was the one he was part of. Do you remember the one Abby Appleby came in on? John was on the same one."

"Why didn't you tell us about him?" Ma asked.

Vicki shrugged. "It just all seemed too special to talk about. I wasn't trying to be mysterious."

"I understand," Ma said. "I was the same way when your father was courting me. My pa thought I was too young to marry, and he told me daily how terrible of a cook I was. I couldn't wait to get out of his house."

"I didn't know that!" Vicki said.

"Well, it's not something I talk about a lot. I just hope you're going to be as happy with John as you think you will."

"I will," Vicki said, knowing it was true. John was the perfect man for her. She was certain of it.

After the pies were out of the oven, she got ready for the dance, wishing she could wear the new dress her mother just made her, but she knew she needed to save it for the wedding.

She put on her church dress, fixed her hair, and pinched her cheeks to give them color, though she knew her ma would be very upset if she knew she was pinching her cheeks that way.

When she heard a wagon in the yard, she took the apple pie and carried it out to the wagon, knowing her mother would take the other pie as their family's offering. Vicki felt the apple pie was her first contribution to a potluck as half of a couple.

John jumped down from the wagon when he saw her and kissed her. He helped her into the wagon and got in beside her. "What are you taking to the potluck?" he asked, nodding at the pie in her hands.

"I made a chicken pot pie for Ma to take, and I made an apple pie for us to take."

He smiled. "Very nice. I feel like I'm contributing now."

"That's how I feel too. This is the first thing I've taken to a potluck as part of a couple, so I made two distinct things."

"Good!" He started down the hill toward the church. "I met up with Elmer King Thursday, and he came right over. All the cabinets are in the kitchen now. All I need to do is get a stove, and I can do that on Monday morning. How about marrying me Monday afternoon?"

She almost squealed with excitement. "I love that idea. I'll tell Ma. I think she's almost done with all the sewing."

"How much sewing can there be?" he asked.

She shrugged. "It's Ma's wedding gift to us."

"I made a simple table, and Elmer is going to make a nicer one and chairs, but we can eat off the one I made until he gets them done. I'm so excited that our wedding is finally happening!"

"Me too. It's so hard to stop when we kiss."

"I'm glad you feel the same way about that as I do. I'm definitely ready to make love with you."

"Good," she said. "We'll do that on Monday evening. Ma is planning a wedding supper after the wedding. I'd be happy for the two of us to go in front of Pastor Jed and speak our vows, but Ma says she wants a real wedding this time. We were just settling in when both Roy and Emma got married, and she feels like she missed out on a lot by not being able to go to their weddings, so ours will be larger, no matter what we want."

He frowned. "You don't want a big wedding?"

She shook her head. "And since we're giving her the wedding date two days before the wedding, there's no way we'll have a big one."

"I like the way you think."

When they got to the church, he took the pie from her and carried it inside. Emma hurried over to her as soon as she saw her with John. "Introduce me to your beau."

Vicki smiled at John. "This is my older sister, Emma. Emma, this is my fiancé John."

"I need to walk down the hill more than I do!" Emma said, snuggling her baby close. "How long have you been seeing each other?"

Vicki laughed softly. "We met when his wagon train came through. It was the same one Abby was part of. We both kept thinking of each other. He moved back here, and we started courting."

"That's fast. When is the wedding?"

Vicki grinned. "We talked about that on the way here. I think we're going to marry on Monday."

"Are we invited?"

"Oh, of course! I'm hoping there won't be too many people there, but you and all the Applebys and our family of course need to be there."

"Well, I'm excited you'll still be close. At least I hope you will." Emma looked at John. "Where's your land?"

"Right on the lake," he said. "I've got the house built, and I'll have a stove Monday morning, so we're marrying Monday evening."

"In a hurry, are you?" Emma asked.

"I remember your hurry when you married Jared, so you get to say nothing," Vicki said. She wanted to stick her tongue out at her sister, but she knew better. Maybe in private, but never in public.

Vicki carried the pie to the table, making certain to put it with the other desserts before going back to stand with John.

Emma was still talking to John. "Do you know what time on Monday?" she asked.

John shook his head. "We haven't had a chance to talk to the pastor yet."

"He's right over there. I'll introduce you."

Emma led John to Pastor Jed and introduced them, Vicki lagging behind. Emma had always been more outgoing than she was. "What's a good time to get you to marry us sometime Monday afternoon or evening?" John asked.

The pastor frowned. "Emma's married."

Vicki laughed. "John and I are marrying."

The pastor looked relieved. "I thought you'd been listening to the Mormon teachings."

"Not at all," John said. "I only want one wife. How would a man keep up with two of them?"

"Don't ask me," Pastor Jed said. "It's all I can do to keep up with Hannah and the children."

"Is there a time that's better than others?" Vicki asked. "My ma is planning on a supper that you and Mrs. Scott are welcome to join us for."

"Let's do it about five then. I'm always happy to give Hannah a night off from cooking. She has her hands full with the children and housework. I honestly don't know how she does it all."

"Five sounds good. Thank you, Pastor," Vicki said, slowly moving away. "Now we just need to tell Ma it's Monday."

"Ma doesn't know the date yet? Have you lost your mind, Victoria Abigail?"

"Nope. Just my heart."

Vicki pulled John away from her sister. "Emma is the oldest sister, as I'm sure you can tell. I never felt that I could live up to her."

"I think most younger sisters feel that way," John said. "Don't worry about it."

Shortly after, Vicki saw her mother walk into the church, and she rushed over to her. "Ma, the house is done. We're getting married at five in the evening on Monday. That will give John time to have my new stove delivered."

Ma nodded. "How many people do you plan to invite?"

"I'm thinking the Applebys, the pastor and Mrs. Scott, and maybe Abby's best friend and her husband. They'll be our closest neighbors. Roy and Henri, of course."

"Sounds good. I can have everything I'm doing ready by then, and if I talk to Henri and Emma, we'll have all the food we need."

Vicki grinned at John. She'd been worried her mother would have a reason that it was too soon for them to marry, and she was glad there was nothing standing in their way.

John nodded. "Thank you for helping with the fast service, Mrs. Williams."

"Oh, just call me Ma. Everyone else does," Ma said.

John smiled. "I'll do that happily, Ma."

Word spread quickly among the family and when Vicki saw Anna walk into the church, she hurried over. "John says we're going to be neighbors, and I just wanted to invite you to the small wedding we're having here at five on Monday evening."

"Oh, we'd love to come!" Anna said. "Abby will be here, right?"

Vicki nodded. "She certainly will."

"Sounds wonderful," Anna said.

Soon it was time for their meal, and they had a group prayer and all the women moved to stand behind what they'd made for the meal. Ma sent Barbara to stand behind the chicken pot pie because they all knew if she stood behind it, no one would dare to eat it.

Once the meal had been served, and eaten, the women made quick work of the dishes, and then the dancing started. Vicki's heart skipped a beat as the band warmed up, and she smiled over at John, who was talking with Mr. Appleby. Hopefully, he was arranging for his hogs.

As her part of the cleanup was over, she joined John, who was indeed talking about hogs. "Mr. Appleby," she said softly.

"Vicki," he said with a smile. "Your young man was just telling me about the wedding on Monday. I hope you two will be happy together, and that your new hogs will be just as happy."

Vicki laughed. "I'm not sure that they're happiness affects their taste very much."

"No, not really, but I still think we should be as kind to them as we can be."

Chapter Seven

As soon as the dancing started, John took Vicki's hand and led her out onto the dancefloor. One room of the church had been built large enough for dances and potlucks and anything else they wanted, and if there was overflow, they'd move the pews to the edges of the room.

He held her close as they danced to a slow song, and then they danced to one much faster, and while her nimble feet could easily keep up with the music, he stomped on her foot more than once. Finally, she took his hand and led him away from the other dancers. "I need to be able to walk down the aisle at my wedding, so I think we're only dancing to slow songs for the rest of the night."

John looked chagrined. "I'm so sorry. I would never intentionally hurt you."

"I'm well aware. I wouldn't be marrying you otherwise." She led him over to a bucket of water, with tin cups to drink from. "I enjoy the fast songs, but we'll have to practice a little more before we can get them perfect."

He nodded. "That's probably for the best. It never occurred to me that there would be faster songs. In my mind, a dance is holding one another and swaying to the music."

"I think I'd like that kind of dance a great deal more with you."

Henri walked over a moment later, a baby in her arms, and a toddler trailing along behind her. "This must be John!" she said. "I'm Henri Williams. I'm married to Vicki's older brother, Roy."

"It's so nice to meet you," he said. "I heard you're responsible for the receipt for the chicken and dumplings that made me so happy the other night."

Henri nodded. "That would be me. It's so easy to teach Ab—Vicki new things. She's a very good student."

"Well, I appreciate the time you've spent teaching her to cook after hearing about the way her mother cooks."

Henri nodded. "Her mother is better now, but she's still not what I would consider a good cook."

"Henri is the best sister-in-law a girl could ask for," Vicki said with a smile. "The only thing I want from you for a wedding gift is receipts."

"I started making you a book full of them when I saw you talking to John back in October. And I'm always willing to help if something is harder than you think it will be."

"And I'll always add the little extra to the dress you're making."

"We make a good team," Henri said.

"We do!" Vicki agreed.

"What do you mean by little extra on dresses?" John asked.

"Embroidery or a lace collar. Ma loves to sew so much, and she's really good, so she taught all of us girls to sew, and we're good at making things extra special."

"Could you make a special lace collar for my ma?" he asked.

She nodded. "I'd be happy to. I'm assuming she would have the skills to sew it onto a dress?"

"Definitely. But she'd probably give the collar to one of my sisters."

"I can make four easily," she said. "And then each of your sisters can have one, but so can your ma. I'll just do each one a little differently, and then they won't look all the same."

"That sounds like a good idea," he said. "If you don't mind, that would make me very happy. My sisters all feel they'll never marry because they don't have pretty clothes. They could dress up anything with a pretty lace collar."

Henri pointed to the lace collar on the baby's dress. "Like little Millie."

"Yes, that's the type of thing I want."

"I can do that with no problem," Vicki said. "I'd be happy to."

"Thank you," he said. "Ma would never accept money or anything like that as a gift, but lace collars, she would definitely accept for her and the girls."

Vicki smiled. "There's a slow song again."

"Would you care to dance with me?"

She nodded. "See you later, Henri."

Henri watched them go to the dancefloor with a longing look on her face, then went to find her mother-in-law to get her to watch her grandchildren while she danced with her husband.

After church the following day, John took Vicki back to the house, so she could see his progress. There were beautiful cabinets in the kitchen, not many because the kitchen was rather small, but it was enough for Vicki's needs. A bed had been moved in and set up against one wall of the room.

"I love it, John. It's just perfect!"

He laughed. "Oh, it's definitely not perfect, but I'm happy if you're happy."

"I am so happy with it. I'll make curtains and a tablecloth, and it will be the most beautiful little home in all of Oregon Territory."

She threw her arms around him and kissed him quickly. "And I want the garden to be right outside the kitchen window, so I can look at it while I'm doing the dishes."

"I'll make sure that gets plowed early in the week, so you can get everything in the ground."

"There's time," she said. "We had an early spring this year, but we don't usually plant until May."

"I see." He glanced over at the bed and realized it may be just a bit too much temptation to have her inside alone with him. "We'd better go," he said.

"Why? We just got here."

"Because temptation is strong. I want to take you to that bed and have my way with you, but I can't do that until tomorrow evening and we've spoken our vows."

She sighed. "I know. I want to do just what you want to do."

"Let's go outside then, and we'll talk about the garden."

"All right. And I want a porch swing," she said. "I know it's a lot to ask, especially since we don't have a porch yet, but a swing to sit on when I need a few minutes in the middle of the day would make me so happy."

He nodded. "I can do that," he said. "You don't want me to wait to build a porch?"

"I don't think there's any way you'll get around to putting up a porch until next summer at the earliest. Just make me a swing, and I'll be happy."

"All right. I can do that." John was determined to do whatever it took to make her happy.

"Do you have a pen and paper?" she asked.

He nodded. "Sure do."

"I want to make a list of what we'll need for the pantry so I can cook. Is that all right?"

"Of course. You're going to be feeding me, right?"

"Yes, I will. Three meals a day every day." She looked around the little house. "Are you already living here?"

"Tonight will be my first night to spend here, and the only night I plan on being alone here. You're going to be here tomorrow night."

She glanced at the bed again. Did one day really matter that much? She knew it mattered to her ma, and she didn't let herself go down that road. No, she was going to be legally married before she made love with him. That was her vow to herself.

John fetched her the paper and a pencil, and she sat down on the little bench and carefully wrote out a list of what she would need. "It's going to be a lot this first trip," she said. "I have pots and pans and dishes, but I don't have any flour or sugar. I have things to cook on but nothing to cook!"

He laughed. "Just give me the list, and I'll pop by the store first thing in the morning to get it delivered with the stove."

"Are you sure they have a stove?" she asked. Vicki had rarely stepped foot into the store. Her ma had gotten into the habit of going alone over the years, and it was something she'd stayed with when they'd settled there.

He nodded. "They had one in the store last week, and I paid for it then. Mr. Jensen is just waiting for me to tell him when I'm ready to have it delivered."

"Wonderful. Then I really will be cooking on it by Tuesday morning."

"Yes, you will."

"Would you mind if I also had a firepit outside? Sometimes it's easier to cook meat over an open fire."

"I don't mind at all. It's your house, and the yard is yours to decide what to do with."

She grinned. "Flowers. Would you mind if I planted flowers in front of the house?"

He shrugged. "Not if they're not too costly," he said. "I'm doing my best not to waste money on frivolous purchases."

"I would never waste money. I could take in sewing if it would help us out financially."

"No, I don't want you working. Just try to be frugal, and I'll be a happy man. I have some extra from mine work, and some of the men on the trail paid me to take their turns watching guard. I was happy to take anything I could get."

"Let me know if you change your mind," she said.

"I will. And I so appreciate your willingness to work. Maybe you could be in charge of the hogs, and we could sell them if we had enough."

"I'm happy to do that," she said. "Whatever it takes. You'll be my family starting tomorrow, and I want to do everything I can to help us."

He smiled. "Tonight, will be my last night sleeping alone," he said softly. "I always had to share a room with my five brothers, and I thought sleeping alone would be the most wonderful thing in the world. Now all I can think about is sleeping with someone beside me. In my arms."

"All I can think about is you slipping inside me. I know I shouldn't be thinking impure thoughts that way, but I cannot wait."

He shuddered. "You're killing me, Vicki. I can wait one more day, can't I?"

"If I can, you can," she said with a smile. "Drive me home and have supper with my family. Then the next time you see me, I'll be the girl walking down the aisle toward you." She handed him the list she'd finished.

"I'll take this with me in the morning. I really do need to take you home, though, or there's no way I'm going to be able to wait another twenty-four minutes, let alone twenty-four hours."

"I love the house. I'm glad you brought me here, but let's get back to my parents' house before we do something stupid."

He didn't have to be told twice. "One last kiss before we go," he said.

"I'm not sure that's a smart thing to do."

"I just have to have one more taste of you."

She went willingly into his arms, wrapping herself around him. His kiss made her feel so much, especially in the core of her body. By the time he let her go, she was tingling all over. "We have to go now!" she said. She knew she wouldn't be able to say no to him again, and she'd made a vow to herself and her mother that nothing would happen before their wedding.

In the wagon on the way back, she sat a proper distance away from him. They never should have started kissing the way they had, but oh, how she was happy they were marrying. One more day. They could both last one more day.

She didn't draw an easy breath until they were in her parents' yard. She knew she would do nothing untoward there. Her parents would never allow it.

She realized as he helped her down that they hadn't really spoken the entire drive back. The air had been too charged with emotion, and more than that, with passion.

When they walked into the house, Barbara was just putting supper on the table. "We weren't sure you were coming back," she said. "I made a cottage pie for supper."

"Oh, that sounds delicious," Vicki said, going into the kitchen to wash her hands in the bucket kept there for that purpose.

"What's a cottage pie?" John asked as he washed his hands as well.

"It's beef that we've put through a mincer, mashed potatoes, peas, carrots, and some sauce. It's absolutely delicious."

"I can't wait to try it," he said. "Do you make cottage pie?"

"I sure do. I absolutely love it."

"I hope you'll serve it often then." He loved how this family had meat with almost every meal, and he hoped they'd be able to carry that on, but as a farmer, he felt he would always have meat on hand. He hoped so anyway.

When they all sat down to supper, Ma smiled at John. "Tomorrow at this time, you'll be our son. Welcome to the family."

John smiled. "Thank you. I can't tell you how proud I am that Vicki has agreed to be my wife."

After the prayer, he tried the cottage pie, and he smiled and nodded. "I may like this more than chicken and dumplings," he said.

"They can be equal in your mind," Vicki countered.

Barbara smiled. "I'm going to be the only daughter still at home. It's going to be wonderful!"

Vicki raised an eyebrow at her sister. "Double chores? I do worry about you sometimes, Barbara."

"I didn't think of it that way."

"Now you can," Vicki said, realizing she was being petty. "But there will be one less person, so the chores will be lighter as well."

Barbara smiled again. "They will! And I know if I beg enough you'll come over and help with the gardening."

"I'll have my own garden to tend to," Vicki said. "I'm so excited to put it in."

"We just finished putting in a garden," Barbara said. "I'm sure you've lost your mind."

John shook his head. "It feels like I'm at home and my sisters are arguing about the chores."

Ma laughed. "These two have always bickered. In a few years, I do think they'll be the best of friends, though."

"Maybe." John didn't care if they were friends or not, as long as Vicki was happy. And he had a feeling that he could easily see to her happiness.

When he left that night, he kissed Vicki lightly. "Save all your kisses for me," he said softly.

"I always have," Vicki said. As she watched him drive away, she realized it was for the last time, because this time tomorrow, she would be his wife, and sleeping in his bed with him.

She shivered a bit, and it had nothing to do with the temperature. She was so looking forward to being his wife.

Chapter Eight

The morning of her wedding, Vicki was up before dawn. She didn't need to be up that early, but her nervous energy was keeping her from sleeping. So she went into the kitchen and mixed up bread dough, thinking they could all have a cinnamon roll with breakfast.

She preferred the pastry still warm, but it meant getting up much earlier than usual, which she had, so she took the time to make their breakfast special. It was the last one she'd cook for her family.

Why that made her feel a bit sad on what should be the happiest day of her life, she wasn't sure. She worked on the meal while humming a tune.

When Ma got up, she stared at Vicki for a moment. "What are you making?" she asked. Usually, Ma took care of breakfast. They did a lot of oatmeal.

Vicki shrugged. "I was too excited to sleep, so I thought I'd make a special breakfast."

Ma, still in her nightgown, sat down at the table. "I see. I guess it's the last meal you'll make for the family."

"I'll make lunch too," Vicki said quickly. "I want to make the most of my last day with you here."

Ma laughed softly. "You make it sound like you're moving across the country. You're going to be a very short drive away."

"I know...but visits won't be the same."

"Are you getting cold feet?"

Vicki sighed, sitting down with her mother as she waited for the cinnamon rolls to rise. "Not really. I'm just very aware that this is my last day living at home. This evening, I'll be going to John's house with him, and when I return, I'll no longer be at my home, I'll be a visitor."

Ma reached out and squeezed her hand. "Do you have any questions for me about the wedding night?"

Vicki chuckled. "Most mothers would be telling their daughter what their duty was to their husband. Not my ma. Do you need advice to make your wedding night better?'

Ma smiled. "No one should go into marriage afraid of her wedding night like I did. What you will do with John will be as enjoyable as you let it be. Some women close their eyes and refuse to acknowledge the fact their husband is trying to make them feel good. I don't want any of my daughters to do that."

"I appreciate that, Ma. I really do. I think John does too. He knows I'm eager for our wedding night, and not afraid. Oh, Ma. It was all I could do to keep my vow to you yesterday. He was showing me our house, and we were alone with a bed right there. Using that bed was all I could think about. We drove slowly back to town because we had to leave to keep from anticipating our wedding vows."

Ma smiled and nodded. "I'm just glad you were able to. Tonight will be much more special because of it."

Vicki nodded. "I think so too."

"Don't expect it to be perfect the first few times. A man needs to learn control, and his first time with his wife, he will have no control at all. Be patient with him, and just love him."

"I'll do my very best," Vicki said. "I do think we're going to enjoy being together."

"Of course, you will. If you enjoy kissing him, then you'll enjoy making love with him. It's as simple as that."

Vicki nodded. "I really enjoy kissing him, so I know my marriage will be a good one."

"There's more to marriage than just making love," Ma said softly. "There's work involved, and it's work you know how to do, but you need to keep it up every day. Just as he'll go to work on the farm, you'll be working to keep the house clean, to cook three meals per day, to plant, weed, water, and harvest a garden, and then spend your time putting up the harvest. You have a vital role in your marriage, and you must make the best of it."

Vicki nodded. "I'll also be in charge of the chickens and pigs," she said, smiling at the thought of the piglets she'd be raising. She would cull only a few each year so they could sell some for meat, but continue to grow.

Ma smiled. "I think that will be your favorite part of your chores. I know you love gardening, but when you get to see those animals grow and take a liking to you, you're going to know that you are doing what you were born to do."

"I hope so, Ma. I really do!"

"You'll love it. I promise. I had your pa make a few boxes to carry your chickens home in. I'm sending a rooster and five good-laying hens for eggs. I think you'll be quite happy. You know what to feed them and how to feed them. Pigs are like chickens, and they'll eat everything in front of them. They'll need a pen, but I think you'll prefer to leave the chickens as free-range. They'll need a henhouse for the winter, but in the summer, they'll eat insects, and you won't have to feed them quite as much. Pigs you'll always have to feed."

Vicki nodded, getting up to put the cinnamon rolls into the oven. "How about eggs, bacon, and cinnamon rolls for breakfast?"

"That sounds wonderful. Thank you for getting up early to cook. It'll make my morning a great deal easier, which is good, because my daughter is getting married today."

"Oh, Ma, I can't wait! I wish it was time now!"

By early afternoon, Vicki was exhausted. All of her things were in the hope chest her father had bought from Elmer King, and it was packed nicely. After the wedding, they would get her hope chest and the chickens out of her parents' wagon and drive straight to the lake and their home.

Everything was ready for the wedding except her. She needed to dress and fix her hair, but she needed to sleep more. She couldn't remember the last time she'd napped, but she knew if she didn't that day, she wouldn't be as attentive and willing for her wedding night.

She found her ma outside watering the garden. Ma looked up. "Everything ready?"

"Everything except me," Vicki said. "Would it be all right if I took a nap? I slept so little last night."

"I know. Go ahead. I'll make sure you're awake in time to dress for the wedding."

"I want to try something new with my hair as well," Vicki said.

"No you don't," Ma replied. "Something new may not look right, and then you'd have to start all over. Pin most of your hair up in a bun, but let a little of it fall free."

"Yes, Ma. I'll do that after I nap." Vicki hid a yawn behind her hand. "I think I should be awake by four or so."

Ma nodded. "I'll wake you."

Vicki went back into the house and sat on her bed, looking around her room. This would be her last time to sleep in this bed. Oh, it was all becoming so real. She'd been dreaming about this day since she met John, and now that it was here, she was ready to do all she could.

She laid on her side and closed her eyes and sleep claimed her quickly.

Ma woke her at four-thirty. "I let you sleep another half hour because I knew you needed it. Change into your dress, and I'll help fix your hair."

Vicki nodded. She could smell chicken and dumplings and realized Barbara must have been cooking them for the wedding supper.

She changed and went out into the dining room, where Ma was sitting, doing a bit of embroidery while she waited. "Does this look all right?" she asked.

Ma looked her up and down and smiled. "It fits you perfectly. You look beautiful today. Your eyes look tired, though. You may want to rest a cool damp rag on them."

"I can do that while you do my hair," Vicki said, hurrying to the kitchen for the damp rag.

While she sat, her mother worked on her hair. "You have an exact look in mind, don't you, Ma?"

"I do. I can just see how it will look, so you sit there patiently and let me have my way. I haven't fixed your hair since you were a little girl."

"I can't remember the last time anyone fixed my hair," she said.

"I have all the chicken and dumplings done," Barbara said. "I know I fixed enough to feed us, Roy and Henri's family, and Emma and Jared's family. I know others are making them too, so I am going to say I've made enough."

"Thanks for helping out with my wedding supper," Vicki said.

"If it gets you out of the house faster..."

"Barbara Ann!" Ma said. "You do not talk to your sister that way."

Knowing her ma was behind her and wouldn't see, Vicki poked her tongue out at her sister, getting a laugh from Barbara Ann. "I get to move into your room tonight," Barbara said. "It's bigger than mine."

"I hope you love it as much as I have," Vicki said. "My whole house isn't as big as the cabin we lived in when we first moved here."

"It's good when there's room to grow," Ma said.

Once her hair was finished, Vicki looked into a mirror and smiled. "That's perfect, Ma. Thank you!" She took the cloth from her eyes. "Now I need to go pinch my cheeks..." she teased.

"On your wedding day, I think that's fine," Ma said to Vicki's surprise.

Vicki smiled. "You're the best ma ever!"

Vicki and Barbara each took one end of her hope chest and carried it outside. "I'm so glad Pa finally got us both hope chests again," Barbara said. "Every time I put something into my hope bag, I was embarrassed for myself and all of humanity."

"Have you ever thought of writing a book?" Vicki asked.

Barbara shook her head. "No, should I?"

"Well, you've certainly mastered the use of hyperbole, and I think that would be quite useful in writing a book."

"You're right. I'll start one tonight." They put the heavy chest down in the yard where Pa would pull the wagon to, so he could load it. "I'm going to miss you, even though you make me crazy."

Vicki smiled. "I'll miss you too. All day, all I've been able to think about was my last times. I cooked breakfast for the last time for my family. I woke up in the morning in this house for the last time. I slept in my bed for the last time. I should be looking to the new times, but I know I'm going to miss working with you and Ma every day."

Barbara nodded, and to Vicki's surprise, her sister hugged her tightly. "I hope you're happy with John. He seems like a good man."

"He is," Vicki said, feeling confident in her statement. "Living on his farm is going to make me very happy. But if you want to come and help me plant later this week…"

"No way!" Barbara said laughing. "You know how much I hate gardening."

"Almost as much as I love it," Vicki said, grinning at her sister. "Isn't it nice that God makes everyone different from everyone else?"

"It is. I hope you'll let me come visit you."

"You're my sister! You can visit every third Tuesday as long as there's a full moon."

Barbara laughed. "I'll keep that in mind."

When Pa got home a few minutes later, he hurried inside. "I need to get cleaned up, and then we'll go."

When he and Ma stepped outside a few minutes later, Vicki was proud of how they looked. Each had taken care with their appearance, and they looked ready to go.

"Father of the bride," Pa said. "Again. Only one more time for my Barbara."

"A long time!" Barbara said. "I'm going to be the happiest only child alive for as long as I can make it work."

Ma laughed. "You'll meet a young man soon enough. There's no doubt in my mind."

"I don't think I will," Barbara said. "I'm happy to be on my own. Maybe I'll be a spinster and make hats. That's what Edna told me she was going to do. I think she'll be good at it too."

"Why would she want to be a spinster who made hats?" Ma asked.

Vicki shook her head. "Edna Blue was a mystery. I don't think I'll ever understand half of what she said and did."

Pa nodded. "Her father was a bit odd, but nothing like that daughter of his. Just the way she danced on Saturday nights told me all I needed to know. She was a halfwit!"

"I don't think so," Barbara said. "She was intelligent, but she simply said strange things all the time that confused everyone around her."

"Maybe," Vicki said.

Instead of climbing into the back of the wagon, her pa helped Ma up and then Vicki. It was cramped on the wagon seat, but Vicki didn't let that bother her. She definitely didn't want to be seen climbing out of the back of the wagon at the church on her wedding day. Sitting in the back had always made her feel as if she was a small child. Now that she was going to be married, she was a grown woman, and she felt others should treat her as such.

She waited for her pa to help her down at the church, and she went into the parsonage, which was part of the church. That way she could do her walk down the aisle, and John wouldn't see her before the wedding. She thought it was a silly superstition, but Ma kept telling her it didn't hurt to be careful.

She also wore something new, her dress. Something blue, a bouquet of wildflowers, something borrowed, her mother's favorite hair comb.

On her feet were her old shoes because they hadn't had time to order new ones. That covered that silly superstition as well.

Vicki cared about none of it. She only cared that she was about to walk down the aisle to the man of her dreams with all her family watching over them. For a moment, she wished Edna could be there to take part in her wedding. She was the best wedding guest, always giving sex advice to the newlyweds. What more could she ask for?

She took a deep breath and started down the aisle on her father's arm. When she walked back down, she would be John's wife. What a glorious day!

Chapter Nine

John turned to her as Vicki walked toward him, her gaze on his face and nothing else. Pastor Jed had a big smile on his face, as he loved performing weddings. He had once said that he preferred funerals because you always knew then how the person's life had turned out, but he was happy to do weddings as well.

When she reached John, and Pastor Jed had asked her father who gave her in marriage, her father placed her hand into John's and they turned to face Pastor Jed together. Vicki had never enjoyed being the center of attention, but John's hand held her steady. He made her feel as if she was the most important thing in his entire world, and truthfully, she was.

When she made her vows, Vicki immediately realized she'd kept the vow she'd made to both her mother and herself. She had not sinned with John.

Then the pastor was proclaiming them man and wife, and John didn't have to be told to kiss his bride. His lips were on hers before the pastor got the words out, and everyone laughed.

Afterward, they went into the other room of the church for their wedding supper, and John was thrilled to see the chicken and dumplings. "Thank you!" he said looking at Vicki, knowing she was the one who had decided to serve them.

"Anything to make you happy," she said softly.

There was no band that evening, so there would be no dancing. Instead, their supper was served in silence, with only the voices of people talking over their meals providing the background music.

The food tasted like sawdust to Vicki, and she wanted to just leave the church with John and go to the little house he built for them and be alone, knowing they were allowed to do what they both wanted so badly.

Her family surrounded them, but she barely noticed. Her eyes were on John and only John. Emma poked her in the side. "There are people here other than your husband," she said.

"But he's the only one I married today, so shush." Vicki turned her attention back to John, who laughed softly.

"I guess I get all the attention today," he said. "You can have attention on another day."

Jared, Emma's husband nodded emphatically. "That's how it should be."

As soon as they felt they could get away without anyone thinking they were escaping too quickly, they headed out to John's wagon. Her father and Roy followed them outside, so they could move the chickens into John's wagon as well as her hope chest.

John offered to help, but Pa and Roy were used to working together and made short work of the job. When they were finished, she hugged her father and brother. "Thank you."

Pa nodded. "Be happy."

"I will!" There was no doubt in her mind that John would make her the happiest woman alive. Once they finally reached the house that was.

"I'm going to drive as fast as I feel comfortable driving," he whispered as they moved off the church lawn and started toward the lake.

"Brilliant idea!" she said.

"I think so," he said, smiling at her. "I'm surprised your parents were so willing to let us get married so quickly. I expected it would take months once I settled here to convince your father."

"Nah. Barbara was practically singing and dancing and celebrating being the only child left at home."

He laughed. "I could tell she was excited about it. Any last-minute advice from you ma?" he asked.

"Actually yes. She thinks I'm putting a bit too much emphasis on the physical side of our marriage, and reminded me that I have plenty of duties outside the bedroom. She made this long list of things I'll be required to do, but none of them are things I haven't already done at home. Well, except for the hogs. When do we get those?"

"They need a few more weeks," he said. "Probably end of June."

"That works for me." Vicki scooted closer to him on the wagon seat. "I cannot tell you how much I have been anticipating tonight."

"You and me both."

She realized then her mother hadn't shown her the nightgown for her wedding night, but she had a feeling it was packed in the back of the wagon somewhere. She'd expected to take her hope chest and the chickens. Instead, there were many extra boxes in the back of John's wagon, and she had no idea what she would find in them. It would be like a treasure hunt, and she knew she'd enjoy it.

"Did you get the stove?" she asked.

He nodded. "And all the other things you asked for. Mrs. Jensen said it looked like I was setting up house, and I told her we were marrying today. She said to tell you best wishes, and if you need anything from her, to let her know."

"She's so sweet," Vicki said. "I'm glad I can call her friend."

When they finally reached the house, she looked in the back of the wagon. "Let me help you get all this unloaded before we do anything else. The chickens have already been cooped up too long, even though we don't have a coop!"

"We will have one just as soon as I finish the barn. Thankfully, there's not a ton to do with such a small herd, but it will grow."

She took the chickens out one at a time and carried them to the area where John planned to build their barn. She knew each of the chickens, and though her mother had never been one to name a bird that would someday end up on their table, she could tell them apart easily. They were hers.

Then she helped with the boxes her mother had added, and she was surprised at how many had been sneaked in without her looking. Someone must have gone home to get more, but she hadn't noticed anyone missing from the supper. Of course, she'd only had eyes for John.

Once he had her trunk inside, he shook his head. "This is a lot more than I thought you were bringing with you."

"I thought I was bringing my hope chest and six chickens. That's all. Instead, I have all these extra boxes with who knows what in them. I'm going to have to dig through them for something before we can go to bed, though." She desperately wanted to wear the nightgown she was certain her mother had made her.

"It can't wait?" he asked.

She shook her head. "It can't. I have to look, and unfortunately, I have to look alone. Could you give me twenty minutes to get ready for bed please?"

He groaned. "I guess I can wait twenty minutes, but after that, I'm not letting anything get in my way."

She smiled. "You know I'm as anxious as you."

He kissed her quickly and left the house, and she worked to open all the boxes her mother had packed. There were some things that thrilled her. A quilt her mother had made for her years before, that had always been intended to cover her marriage bed, and she quickly spread it out on the bed that had one thin blanket on it. It brightened up the whole house.

In another box, she found not only jerky but salt pork and some of the meats she'd helped can the fall before.

In another, she found a note from her pa that was folded closed with John's name on it. She wanted to look, but she knew it was rude to read someone else's mail.

Finally, in the last box, she found the nightgown. She quickly pulled her dress over her head and divested herself of her underwear, pulling on the nightgown. Then she looked down at herself, and she could easily see her nipples and the shape of her breasts through the lace of the bodice. She had a feeling John may never let her wear anything else once he saw her in that.

While she waited, she put the note for John on the table, and she put the food into the kitchen. She'd probably carry it down to the cellar later, but for now, it was good enough.

As she removed things, she immediately put them where they belonged, and all at once, the bare house seemed to transform into a home. She was very pleased with all she'd accomplished when John opened the door.

"I hope you're ready because I'm not sure how much longer I can wait," he called as he opened the door.

She turned from what she'd been doing and stood before him in the nightgown her mother had made. His jaw dropped at the sight of her. "Where did that come from?"

"My ma made it special for our wedding night." She knew she should feel embarrassed at how see-through the thing was, but it made her feel good to see the desire so clearly on his face. She spun in a small circle. "Do you like it?"

"I'm not sure like is the right word," he said gruffly. He walked across the small room and took her in his arms. "Your mother is something special."

Vicki grinned. "It's nice, isn't it?"

He nodded, staring at her for a moment, before lowering his head to kiss her. She wore the thing for less than ten minutes, but it had done its job beautifully. He pulled it over her head, and she unbuttoned his shirt, needing him to be as naked as she was.

As she struggled to get him out of his clothes, his hands moved all over her. One moment cupping her breasts, and then next pulling her into him by her bottom. She shook her head. "If you could hold still for just a moment, we could get these clothes off you, and it would be much faster."

Abruptly he dropped his hands to the waist of his pants, unbuttoning them. "I'm all for fast."

Within moments, they were on the bed, and their hands were all over each other. When she reached down to touch him where she'd never touched a man before, he groaned. "I like that a little too much."

"Why too much?"

"Because if you don't stop, there will only be fun for me and none for you."

She giggled. "We can't have that now, can we?"

"No, we cannot."

When he covered her body with his, he reached a hand down to guide himself inside her. She made a sound, but even she wasn't sure if it was pain or pleasure, as the two had seemed to merge together in that moment.

When he was deeply inside her, he held still for a moment. "I think you said something about not being able to wait until I could slip inside you?"

She moaned softly. "And I was right. That feeling is like nothing else."

When they had finished, she moved toward him and rested her head on his shoulder. "That was nice. We should do it again sometime."

He laughed. "Maybe in an hour or two."

"That would be nice."

He sighed happily. "I'm so glad you agreed to marry me, and not just because it feels so incredible to be inside you."

"Is that so?" she asked, leaning on one elbow as she watched him.

"Yup."

"There was a note addressed to you in one of the boxes I unpacked," she said. "I didn't read it because my name was not added."

"Where did you put it?" he asked.

"On the table."

"There's no way I can get up and go read it. I may never be able to move again." He kissed her softly. "Marriage is amazing."

She laughed. "The first few hours are absolutely perfect." She climbed out of bed and walked across the room to fetch the letter, wondering what it was all about. She handed it to him, and only then did she realize they'd forgotten to blow out the candle. One of them would have to be responsible and not waste candles.

He sat up in bed. "You didn't have to get it," he said.

"I was curious about it. Someone in my family must have written you a note and I was not included. I need to know what it said!"

He read the note and smiled. "Your pa and Mr. Appleby are giving us six heifers each. And they are all expecting, which means twenty-four new cows for our little dairy farm."

Vicki smiled happily. "Oh, that's wonderful, John! Did he say when?"

"Your father and Roy plan to drive them here at the end of the week. That's going to take a while." He shook his head. "I think we'll have overnight visitors one night."

She sighed. "We'll have to enjoy each other a great deal before they get here so we won't be so lonely for each other," she said.

"I'm all for it," John told her.

"I noticed you plowed the space for my garden already. Have I told you how much that means to me"

He shook his head. "No, you haven't. Shame on you."

"Well, it means that I can get out there tomorrow and start digging in the dirt. I find nothing in this world more soothing than being outdoors."

"And cooking for your husband, right?"

"Well, of course," she said. "Ma sent a bunch of jerky, and some other meats that I helped put up last fall, so we'll be set on meat for a while. I wasn't expecting that, but there it was in one of the boxes."

"That's good," he said. "Will save us time and money, and there's not a lot of either our first summer on the farm."

"Are you sure you don't want me to take in some sewing to help out with the finances?" she asked.

He shook his head. "If it needs to happen later on, I'll let you know, but for now, I'd like to be able to support my wife."

"Make sure you do let me know if something comes up," she said.

"I'll spend tomorrow morning setting up the house, and then tomorrow afternoon I'll start planting the garden. I'm so excited to have my own garden, and Ma sent a bunch of seeds as well. My parents didn't do any of this for Emma and Roy, but they had just finished on the trail back then. They didn't have the extra to give them."

"Guess we got married at the right time," he said.

"We did. I don't want Pa and Roy staying in the house, but I don't think we have a better option for them."

"I don't think so either. It's fine."

"All right. Will you be eating lunch with me?"

"There may be times when I have to take my lunch with me when I leave in the morning, but for the most part, I'll be eating with you."

"Oh, good." She snuggled back down beside him, happy as a clam. Marriage was everything she'd dreamed it would be.

Chapter Ten

When the cows were delivered Friday, Vicki had made a large meal to share with her father and brother. They brought the cows in, and then Pa said, "We're going to head straight back. Neither of us wants to be burdens on your newlywed games."

Vicki laughed. "I cooked supper. I have a beef stew ready to eat right now with fresh bread. Can't you stay for at least that long?"

Pa and Roy exchanged a look. "That jerky we had for lunch sure didn't last."

"Sit," Vicki said. "It'll only take me a minute to get it on the table."

Hearing the sounds of the extra cows, John came in from his work on the barn. "Thank you so much," he said. "I can't think of a better wedding gift for a dairy farmer."

"These cattle weren't bred for dairy, so they may not give as much as the others, but I think anything will help in the beginning," Pa said.

"I'm thrilled to have them," John said, washing his hands and sitting down just as Vicki put the bowls and fresh bread on the table.

After a quick prayer, they tucked into the food, eating quickly. Pa and Roy each had two bowls, and when Vicki asked if they wanted more, they said they needed to get back. "Thanks again to both of you," Vicki said. "It was a very generous gift, and we appreciate it."

"Yes, we do," John said, standing to walk them to the door.

"Now that you have more cows are you going to be too busy for your wife?"

John laughed. "I could never be too busy for the most beautiful wife I have."

"Is that so?"

He nodded.

"Well, you sit right there while I do the dishes, and then we can play more newlywed games as Pa calls them."

"Instead, I'm going to go milk the heifers they just brought. I know they didn't have time to do it after they got here. They sure were in a hurry."

"They didn't want to interrupt us," Vicki said with a smile. "It's nice to have family members who try to support you in all you do."

"It sure is," John said. He kissed her quickly. "Back after I get done milking."

He came back thirty minutes later with a full pail of milk. "There's good cream on this," he said. "Do you want me to put it with the rest of the milk, or do you want to make it into butter?"

"Oh, it's time for me to make butter for sure. You don't have a churn, do you?"

"I'll make you one in the morning."

"Sounds good to me. I could use a few hours off from housework anyway." She wiped the last dish dry and put it into the cabinet. "I love the cabinets you made me."

"I'm glad you find them handy," he said.

"They're wonderful." She stepped outside and looked at the road her pa and brother had left down. "They're gone. Let's get naked."

"Sometimes I think you only love me for my body," John said, trying to sound annoyed.

She laughed. "No...But I do love your body."

He frowned as he realized that she had yet to tell him she loved him. Why hadn't she said the words? She acted as if she loved him, which was good, but if she didn't say how she felt, how would he ever know?

"I love you," he said softly.

She stood on tiptoe and kissed him. "Thank you." She didn't know what else to say because she wasn't yet certain if she did love him.

Nothing had clobbered her over the head and told her she loved him, so she couldn't say the words back. Not in good conscience anyway.

"Don't you love me?" he asked, frowning at her.

She sighed. "I hoped this wouldn't come up until I was sure. I love your body. I love being married to you. I love our life together, but I'm not sure I love you. Hopefully, I'll be sure soon, but I don't want to say it until I'm absolutely certain."

He gaped at her. "You married me without loving me?"

"I can't imagine my life with anyone else, so yes, I married you without loving you. I choose to stay with you, and if anyone has my heart, it's you. But I can't say the words until I'm sure."

"I don't even know how to react to that," he said, his face full of sadness. "I'm going to take a walk."

"I'll come with you!" Vicki said, ready to follow him anywhere.

"No, I think I'd rather be alone for a while."

Vicki busied herself while he was gone, scrubbing the floor and washing down walls that hadn't been there long enough to be dirty. She wondered if she should have said she loved him, just to make him happy, but then she wouldn't have been true to herself. She'd made a vow to love and cherish him, and she was cherishing him, and she was working on loving him. Why wasn't that enough?

She kept working, only realizing when she started to take the stove apart to clean it that he'd been gone much longer than he should have been. She stepped outside and called him as loudly as she could. "John!"

She heard a muffled sound, and she followed it, around the house and into the construction area he called a barn. She found him buried under some boards. "What happened?" she asked, but there was no answer.

She pulled the boards off of him one by one, not caring if they landed in a nice pile. Finally, she had him completely uncovered. "Are you all right?" she asked.

His eyes opened and he blinked at her. "Vicki?"

"You've had some sort of accident," she said. "I've got the boards off you. Can you walk?"

"I don't know." He sat for a minute, trying to decide if there was pain. "My head hurts, but that's all."

"Let me help you up," she said, worried that his head injury could be worse than they realized. "I'm going to hitch up the team and drive you into town to see the doctor."

He shook his head, realizing his mistake when it started hurting more. He put his hand to his head. "No doctors. Just get me home."

With her arm around his waist and his around her shoulders, they hobbled their way back to the house. Once she had him in bed, she asked, "Are you sure I can't take you to see the doctor?"

"I'm sure. I'm just glad you found me."

"Were you working on the barn when it was almost dark?" she asked, thinking the man was a complete idiot for doing something so foolhardy.

"I was. I figured I could get some of my annoyance out by pounding nails."

"You scared me half to death. Don't you realize that you're the reason I get up in the mornings? You go out there and act the fool, and leave me here worried about you? I don't know what I'd do if I lost you!"

He stared at her for a moment, a slow smile crossing his face. "You do love me, don't you?"

"I don't know!" she shouted. "You tried to kill yourself before I could even figure it out!"

His smile turned into a full grin. "Get me a cold rag for my head, would you?" Now that he was certain she loved him, he didn't mind if she took some time to figure it out for herself.

She got the rag and gently put it on his head, washing the blood away. "What were you thinking?" she asked. "I was in here scrubbing an already clean house from top to bottom and you were outside building a barn without sufficient lighting. Even if you were mad at me, how was that at all constructive?"

He shrugged, and just kept grinning that silly grin. She was mad enough at the moment to slap it off his face. "Stop grinning at me, you lunatic."

He laughed. "Come to bed with me," he said, catching her hand and pulling her down atop him.

"We can't do anything while you're too addle-brained to pay attention to anything I'm saying."

"It's my head I hurt not my...middle leg."

"I'm not risking any of you. You can wait til tomorrow."

"To slip inside you?" he asked, pulling her down to sit beside him on the bed. "Now it's all I can think about. How it feels when your body closes around me. How your nipples taste against my tongue. Make love with me, Vicki."

She shook her head adamantly. "I'll sleep in the bed with you, but nothing is going to happen tonight. I'm not risking losing you so you can feel better."

"I love you, Vicki."

She sighed. "I love you too, you idiot."

"Next time leave off calling me an idiot, and I'll be so happy."

"Next time don't be an idiot." She curled up on the bed beside him, not removing any of her clothes for fear he'd talk her into something she shouldn't do. "I was so worried." At that moment the dam broke, and she began to sob. "I could have lost you!"

"But you didn't. I'm fine. My head just hurts a little."

"It should with that giant lump on it." She sniffled again. "Don't ever do that to me again."

"I won't. I promise you that."

"I do love you, John. Even though you're an idiot. Was that better?"

"You could drop the word idiot completely," he said.

"Not for a while yet." She kissed his cheek. "I need you."

Epilogue

Three years later, their herd of cattle had become too much for him to handle alone, and he'd had to hire a younger man to help him out.

Vicki was expecting their second child, and she was so excited she could just burst. They had a little boy, who was named after John, but they called him Jack. Jack was an adorable child, and he filled her heart with gladness every day.

John still had a small scar from his run-in with the barn, but he had suffered no long-term effects from his idiocy.

Soon, she hoped to have daughters, whom she could tell about how wonderful a wedding night should be. They would love working in the garden, sewing, and cooking. At least she hoped they would. Jack certainly enjoyed helping her weed the garden, but mostly because it gave him time to play in the dirt.

Hopefully, Barbara would find love soon. She'd like to see her sister happily married and having a family of her own. With as many wagon trains coming through as there were, she was sure to meet someone.

Her life was perfect in her eyes, even though she'd long since realized her husband was not. John made her crazy at times, but she loved him with everything inside her. Love had been the real goal. Not marriage.

Milton Keynes UK
Ingram Content Group UK Ltd.
UKHW040638131123
432470UK00001B/142